TALES OF THE DOOMED

FIFTEEN STORIES OF SUFFERING AND DEATH

LEN M. RUTH

TRIGGER WARNINGS

Bondage, dub-con, amateur surgery, cannibalism, mental illness, suicide, terrorism, bombing, hell, references to sexual assault (not depicted), child death, gaslighting, forced feeding, animal death, poisoning, gore, giant cockroaches...

Tales of the Doomed

The story "Sinister Hand" was first published in the anthology *Satan Rides Your Daughter* by HellBound Books Publishing LLC.

The story "Inferno" was performed at San Jose's Flash Fiction Forum on March 10, 2021. Check out this wonderful storytelling venue here: https://www.flashfictionforum.com/

INTRODUCTION

I did not expect to find a theme while looking through my collection of misfit tales, but find one I did. Each of these stories features a character, or characters who are totally screwed. And just like that, the title for this collection materialized.

I hope you enjoy reading these stories as much as I enjoyed writing them and presenting them to you. Thanks for your continued support.

Len M. Ruth
11/25/2021

ACKNOWLEDGMENTS

For Em

This book is not a solo effort, though I wrote all of its contents. I wish to thank my partner Em, whose love and support keep me going day in and day out.

CONTENTS

RAVENOUS

B arbra ran a manicured finger around the rim of her highball glass and sighed. The Portiere Arriere Hollywood featured hot and cold running cocaine in the bathroom, lighting designed to flatter aging debutants and trophy wives, and a selection of some of the most expensive alcohol products available. She sighed as she looked around—mannequins with enough plastic and silicone to build a Tesla with their recycled parts. The Hollywood elite drank here with no fear of molestation from fans or paparazzi. They were thus free to molest each other in peace.

Barbra graduated Magna Cum (very) Loudly at USC a few years earlier with a degree in Sports Medicine, and a taste for men. Her day job, mothering movie stars with pulled muscles, financed her nightlife nicely and allowed her to hunt for the right men in the right places. Her needs were so prolific and immediate that she'd purchased a van and appointed it nicely. No fucking around in hotel rooms, just get in the van, do the deed, and get on your way.

Tonight, Barbra had her eye on a fine specimen, tall and chiseled in a black tailored suit, dark skin (booth tanned, not spray on), and teeth so bright it hurt to look at them. She didn't like his eyes—small blue dots set too close together. They were so tiny that until he'd looked directly at her and raised a subtle finger, acknowledging her interest, she wasn't sure if he had eyes at all. It didn't matter. It wasn't his eyes Barbra was interested in.

No doubt he'd come over in about two minutes to sit in the empty seat beside her; they all did. She continued to study him, making sure he was this evening's correct selection. No ring, and no tan line on the finger. If he had a lover, she wasn't here with him.

The smell of expensive cologne introduced itself first, musky, overbearing, and vaguely astringent. He sat, and without preamble, flashed a snow-blind cock-sure smile. "Hi, I'm Kenneth."

The direct approach. So rare these days. His lack of a stupid pickup line threw her off for a moment. "Barbra." She took his hand and gave it a firm shake.

"Can I call you Barbie?"

"Only if you want me to cut off your dick and eat it in front of you. Can I call you Ken?" She gauged his reaction.

Nothing for a moment. Then that smile again. "A real man-eater, eh?"

"It would have been funnier if you hadn't taken so long to think it up. Half-points." She smiled, flipped her hair, and took a drink.

"I'll try harder."

"I'm counting on it." She let the corner of her mouth turn up. Then darted her eyes to him, just long enough to be sure he saw her do it, then back to her glass.

"So, are you with anyone tonight?" He leaned an elbow on the bar with practiced nonchalance.

"Not yet." This time she looked into those beady little blue marbles and gave him the full smile.

"Do you want to get out of here?" He set his drink on the bar.

God damn. Fast mover. Normally Barbra liked the banter, the anticipation, the tension, but tonight she was ravenous for what Kenneth had under his suit. "Let's go."

He opened the door for her. "My place is just a couple miles down the road."

"My place is closer," she said, taking his hand and leading him to the parked van around the corner.

"A van?" he looked at her like she was crazy.

"Wait till you see," she winked. She unlocked the back with her fob, then held the door open for him. "After you."

When he'd crawled into the darkness, his feet crinkling on the plastic, she climbed in after him and pulled the door shut.

"What the fuck is this? Why is there plastic over everything?"

"I like it messy, Ken. And I like to be on top." She pushed him onto his back and kissed him. Her hands found his wrists and guided them into the restraints bolted to the floor. Snap, snap.

"Hey, what the fuck?" Ken's struggles were half-hearted.

"You've never been tied up?" Barbra stood, flipped on some mood lighting, and slipped out of her dress. She wasn't wearing anything underneath. She put a hand to her sex, lingered there, then ran it up her body, pausing to circle a nipple with her index finger. It had the calming effect she'd hoped for, and Ken lay still as she slipped her dress into a plastic bag.

"Why are you taking those off?" Ken asked, as her earrings and necklace followed her dress into the bag.

"I told you I like it messy."

"What? Golden showers or something?"

"Not golden." She smiled, then bent over, facing away from him so that he could see from Christmas to New Years. She had his legs in the restraints before he could tear himself away from the view to protest.

"Hey! Seriously? Barbra, I don't like this."

She turned, straddling him. His erection pressed against her.

"You talk too much. In fact, I have the feeling you're a screamer." In one deft motion, she stuffed a rag in his mouth.

Kenneth choked and gagged.

"Too deep? I bet you don't hear that a lot." A layer of duct tape then sealed the rag in place. "There. Now let's see what we're working with, mister." She unbuttoned his shirt with growing anticipation, licking her lips. It was as she'd hoped: chiseled, sculpted, magnificent abs. The skin was smooth on her tongue, untainted by his cologne. Perfect. She opened his shirt and coat as wide as they would go, then fished a scalpel from behind the plastic curtain—three quick slices in the shape of a capital I.

Kenneth screamed into the rag. His body flexed under her. Working quickly with the speed and precision of a butcher, she opened his chest cavity like a basement bulkhead. She took the bolt cutters from behind the plastic beside her—squeeze, crack, so. She held the bone to her lips and sucked at the oozing jagged end.

"Oh, my god, Ken, I was so fucking hungry for ribs."

FOLLOW THE STRING

W ill made his way down the hall, one hand sliding along the peeling wallpaper, the other along a length of twine. The voice called out in a sing-song tone: *follow the string to get to the kitchen—follow the string.*

The abyss reached out from the other side of the hall, clawing and scratching for Will. The wall under his hand was normal enough; he could feel that. The old wooden floorboards creaked under his feet, as they should, but the other wall, the left wall, didn't exist. Where the wall and door should be, an endless dark chasm yawned away into outer space. Will kept tight to the wall that *did* exist. His shoes bumped it with each step. *Follow the string. Follow the string.*

The threshold separating wooden hall from kitchen linoleum met his sole. And two steps later, cold metal met his fingers—the drawer pull at the end of the string. He scrabbled around the counter with shaking hands. It should be here. Should be right here. "Where are my pills?" he pleaded to the silence. His voice sounded strange in his ears. Did he always sound like that? *Follow the string.*

Find the pills. The silence drew so close about him he could feel its breath. Where's the string? Not holding the string. Not holding the string! He reached into his pocket and pulled out his phone.

"Siri, Call Jen." His hands shook.

Siri didn't respond, but he heard Jen's voice. *Will, oh thank G —*

"I'm blind! I... I can't find my... I'm—"

Calm down, Will. Deep breaths, in and out.

Will took several deep breaths.

Better?

"Yes, I... Yes, I'm better."

Good. Did you follow the string?

"Yes, but the pills are gone!"

You told me you took the last one, Will. There's a bottle of whiskey on the counter. I want you to take two big shots.

"Why do you want me to drink? I can't drink near the edge!"

You need a sedative, and the whiskey's all you've got.

"But I let go of the string."

Reach your hand out. What do you feel?

Will reached out. His fingers met the cold, chipped surface of the counter. "It's the counter."

See? You haven't moved. Now, feel around for the bottle.

"Got it."

Good. Now, two big belts, right now.

"Okay." Will uncapped the bottle. One big swallow. The whiskey burned all the way down. Another swallow, bigger than the first. "Ugh, god. Okay."

Okay, Will, repeat after me: I am real. My apartment is real.

Will repeated her words, imitating her soothing tone.

The string is real, Jen pressed on without giving Will time to protest.

"The string is real," Will repeated.

My blindness is not real.

"I can't see—"

My blindness is not real, Jen insisted.

Will sighed. "My blindness is not real."

Good. The abyss is not real.

6

"But I can seeeeee it!"

How can you see it if you are blind?

"Even a blind man can see the abyss!"

How? Will, if you are blind, how can you see it?

She had a point. No denying it. He could see the abyss stretching into forever. Because… "It's so close, so cold. I…"

Follow the string, Will.

"Follow the string. What's happening, Jen?"

You are alone and out of medication. You've got to keep yourself together. You can't go outside.

The quarantine, he'd forgotten. Death outside the door. On the other side of the abyss. The abyss. "You said the abyss isn't real."

No, Will, it isn't. It's all in your mind.

"I need to go outside. I need my pills. I have to go get pills."

Calm down for me, just like in the hospital.

"How—how long have I been alone?"

Best not to think about it.

"Is this real?"

Is what real?

"Talking to you. Is it real?"

Silence.

"It's not real, is it? Your voice… none of it is real."

Follow the string, Will. The string will remind you what's real.

"Follow the string." Will pocketed the phone and grabbed the string, following it hand over hand. The floorboards moaned under his feet as if wounded by his steps. He kept to the wall. One bad step and he'd slide across the hall and tumble into the swirling angry nothingness. In the living room, Will's breathing eased with the portal to eternity, the abyss, behind him. He followed the string to the tall lamp. From lamp to bedroom door-knob. Doorknob to nightstand. Will sat on the bed and ran his fingers along the quilt's stitching. "The quilt is real. The bed is real. My blindness isn't real."

The edges of Will's vision cleared, and as he breathed, the dark spot in the center receded to a single point and disappeared.

Afternoon sunlight filtered through the sheer curtains. Will pulled them aside. No sound from the street below penetrated the window glass—because there was no sound. Nothing moved. No people. No cars. Will let the curtain go and sat back on the bed. He looked at the knot holding the string to the bedside table. There, on the table above the string, a paper. Will picked it up and read:

Lakeview Psychiatric Hospital discharge instructions.

You must take your antipsychotic medication at the same time every day. Failure to take your medication could mean your return to Lakeview.

Call your caseworker if you have any problems. Your caseworker is Jennifer Morton.

Will took the phone from his pocket and pushed the home button. Nothing. He plugged the phone into the charger on the table. Nothing. He looked around the room at the power light on his TV, and the computer. No lights. No screens. No power.

"The power's out, Jen. The phone is dead. So... so I have to ask, are you..."

No. I'm dead. Everyone is dead. How do you like that? Her voice changed as she spoke, from sweet and patronizing, to something older, sinister, and malevolent, as if someone taught a tornado to speak.

This thing talking to him wasn't Jen, wasn't real, couldn't be. Yet there was no one else to check him. No one to balance his impression of reality. "H-how long have I been alone?"

You were always alone... always.

"Do you think it's safe to go out?"

You'd better not, Will. You'd. Better. Not.

"Oh, God." The weight of fear and loneliness consumed him. His vision receded. "I'm going blind again!"

Follow the string.

CURSE IN DISGUISE

I scooted my ass side to side a bit, trying to carve out a comfortable divot in the sharp gravel of the train yard. The light from my fire flickered into the overhanging pines of the verge and disappeared into the chill New England night. To the east, the first pale rays of dawn threatened to overtake the stark horizon of steel train cars.

I pulled a half-smoked cigarette from my pocket, lit it with a half-burnt twig from the fire, and regarded the resulting puff of white smoke with half-mast eyes. Then, I dreamed the American Dream while laying back on my pack and staring straight up at the purple predawn sky. Chubby wife, cute baby, cheap real estate, expensive wine, white picket fence, sex dungeon. The usual.

The crunch of footsteps pulled me from my drowsy reverie. I slid into one pack strap in case I had to run. Yet, I wasn't especially concerned. The approaching footsteps didn't have the purposeful stride of an angry railroad cop. Instead, the inbound stranger came toward the fire at a saunter. And when at last she emerged from the obscurity of the predawn darkness, my breath caught in my throat. For this young woman was a vision of perfection, carved from the purest soapstone. Her clothes, worn and comfortable, didn't belong on the back of a young woman in a train yard. They belonged, the stir in my crotch told me, on the floor of a by-the-hour hotel room.

"Hi. Mind if I share your fire?" Her easy, charming smile was as perfect as her oval moon face, ringed in a halo of curls peeking out from under a black watchman's cap.

"Uh... sure." So smooth. Almost hard to believe I'm single.

Her smile widened a notch. "Thanks."

I drank in every little motion as she folded her perfect denim-clad body into a cross-legged perch.

I opened my mouth to make conversation, but only managed to croak, "uhhh."

"I'm Lucy." She raised a hand, palm out, but did not extend it across the fire.

"Jake." Mesmerized as I was with Lucy's beauty, I couldn't shake the feeling that she didn't belong here.

"You don't belong here either," Lucy said. "No one does. We are universal beings. We are meant to have everything we want. That's what God wants. That's what God's plan for us is. You didn't live your plan."

"How do you know?"

"No one wants to die sitting in the cold hard gravel, freezing their ass off, waiting for a freight train to New Jersey."

"Maybe *I* do." I said it just to be contrary. A Pavlovian response triggered by the words 'God' and 'plan' used in combination.

"Bullshit," Lucy grinned a big, delicious grin. "Come on, what's your dream? If you could have one thing in the whole world, what would it be?"

I gave her my stock, glib answer. "Daily sex with a woman who understands me."

Lucy laughed, her skin reddening visibly in the firelight. "That's a good one. I like that. You could have that, you know."

"I'd settle for a little whiskey." I tossed the butt of my cigarette into the fire.

"You can have that too." She produced a shining stainless flask from inside her thick flannel. Her smile grew unnaturally wide, threatening to touch her temples.

I drew back, scooching away from the fire.

"Easy friend." Lucy uncapped the flask even as her fingers morphed into talons, the nails turning black and pointed. Thick red horns poked through her cap, curled up, and threatened to touch above the center of her head. "Don't look so scared. It's just whiskey."

"You're the Devil!" I tried to rise and run, but some unseen force glued me to the ground.

"Please," she said, "just Lucy. Or Lucy Ferrrr." She rolled the R and locked a white-fanged smile on me at the same time. "It used to be Lucy F-i-r, but I changed the spelling after my clubbing-baby-seals vacation last year. And 'The Devil' is so formal, don't you think? I mean, if we met in my office... but I digress. I'm in a position to offer you anything you want. No strings attached."

"Yeah," I said. "I've seen this movie. This is the one where I sign over my soul, and you screw me."

"It's not like that at all," Lucy said. "I wasn't kidding earlier. God wants you to live in abundance. You are meant to have everything you want."

"Bullshit! You're the Devil—"

"—Lucy—"

"—the uh..." I looked her lithe form up and down "... father... of lies?"

"See! Doesn't fit at all. Totally outdated, outmoded, patriarchal, gender-biased, hetero-normative..."

"What?" All I was thinking about a few minutes ago was getting laid regularly. And now the Devil showed up with all this woke lingo.

Lucy pinched the bright red bridge of her nose with black claws. "Nevermind. The point is, I have to tell you the whole truth when we sign a deal. I also have to give you a thirty-day service agreement."

"The hell you say."

"I never say hell," Lucy said, "there's no such place."

"Okay, hold on, how can you, who are obviously the Devil, sit there and tell me hell doesn't exist?"

Lucy laughed, long and loud. "Oh," she breathed, "wow, that was fantastic. I haven't laughed like that since breakfast. Silly, silly man. I said there's no such place. I never said it didn't exist."

"I don't understand?"

"With the miniaturization technology combined with much greater and universal access to both sin and spiritual enlightenment, we have far more elegant and portable solutions available. But let's not beat that dead horse. We're here to talk about how I can improve your afterlife."

Did she just say, "Afterlife?"

"Yeah," she pointed.

I followed her finger, only to find I was sitting beside myself. My other-self was reclining on my backpack, dead eyes staring up at the stars. "What happened?"

"You froze to death."

"In front of a fire?"

"Sucks huh?" she examined her claws, picked at something, then returned her attention to me. "So, it's daily sex with a woman who understands you?"

"In a nice house. The American Dream. Don't fuck me around on this. I've heard stories. I'm not talking about a crack whore in a burned-out Detroit tenement."

"Wow," the she-devil said, "and I thought *my* world view was bleak. Anyway, as I said, you have a thirty-day service contract. Anything you need, anything that isn't to your satisfaction, any questions, you just pick up the phone and give me a jingle. Then, I come to fix it."

"And that's hell? I'm assuming, since I'm not talking to an angel or St. Peter."

"Don't believe everything you read." Then she smiled, putting a hand to her mouth in a stage whisper. "Especially Deuteronomy, what a load of horseshit." She dropped her hand. "The point is that there is no hell. No heaven either. There is only the afterlife. We all work together as a team to bring you the best in afterlife experiences."

"The last part sounds like a poster in a demon's breakroom."

"Thanks. I wrote it myself. And if demons took breaks, I'd make sure that poster was hanging over the microwave."

I have ADD. This means that sometimes the salient points sail right by, and I grab onto the banality. In this case, my mind skipped right over the fact that I'm dead and instead latched on to: "you have microwaves in… the afterlife?"

"It's all we have. That's why I come to Earth so much. Honestly, it's for the carbs. Ever tried to make bread in a microwave?"

"…um…no."

"Well, don't. Come on," she said, getting to her hooves, "let me show you to your situation."

I rose, trancelike, taking only a cursory notice of my rapidly cooling earthly vessel staring up at the stars with a blank, idiotic expression.

Lucy walked into the night and disappeared ahead of me.

I trotted to keep up and found myself suddenly jogging on a suburban middle-class street on a sunny afternoon. Lucy walked beside me, easily matching my pace.

"Jogging?" I looked down at my designer tracksuit. I'd never worn horrible shit like that in life. Nor had I ever jogged, except to get away from the police.

"You need to keep fit if you're going to have sex every day."

"Right," I said.

"That's your house," she pointed to a huge federal-style mini-mansion.

"Nice!" I said, wondering if my afterwife was already inside waiting.

"No," Lucy said, "because she's pivotal to our deal. You have to pick her out yourself." She produced a phone from nowhere and handed it to me.

The logo said 'Kindling.' I gave her a questioning look.

"It works the same as Tinder. Just swipe."

I tapped the screen. A woman called Susan whooshed into existence as if someone had pushed her through a door from another dimension. The brunette, resplendent in a housecoat and curlers, dropped her eyeliner pencil on the pavement and stared angrily. I tapped her profile to get more information.

"You wanna know about me?" Susan put a hand on her hip and pointed at me with a cigarette I swore hadn't been there a moment earlier. "You can't just swipe me into—" the freshly vaporated brunette began.

"Nope." I swiped left.

A hook appeared, grabbed her by the hips, and yanked.

"Woah!" was all Susan could manage before she evaporated rapidly to the left.

"So, a strong, self-assured woman isn't your thing?" Lucy raised an eyebrow. "That's not what I saw in your mind. Remember. This is the afterlife. Eternal life. Choose carefully."

I tapped the infernal phone again.

A Romanesque brunette materialized from the right, as if someone threw her from a moving car. "Oof!" she exclaimed. Thrusting her hands out to steady herself.

I preferred partners with a little padding and asked this woman, whose name displayed as Marsha, a few questions.

"Seriously, what the hell? One minute—" Marsha began.

"—Not hell. Not exactly." Lucy interrupted. She smiled, much the way sharks smile.

Marsha stared. "You're the Devil!" She raised a shaking finger at Lucy.

"Actually, it's Lu—"

"Yeah, can we do introductions later?" I frowned at Lucy, then turned to Marsha. "Pizza or Tacos?"

"What?" Marsha knit her brows to cover the entire space between them. "What the hell are you talk—"

Lucy raised her devil-claw-fingers and pointed them at Marsha. Then she shouted, "FIVE, FOUR, THREE—"

"Pizza!" Marsha yelled.

Lucy dropped her fingers.

"Cool trick," I said. "What happens when you get to zero?"

"Best you not find out." She winked.

I returned my attention to Marsha. "Cookies or cake?"

"Who fucking cares," Marsha said. "What the fuck is going on here? Why are we standing in the middle of the street?"

I swiped left.

As before, a giant hook materialized out of the air and yanked her away with a:

"What the fuuuu-uuc—"

Next came Kaylee. She sat cross-legged in the road, wide-eyed but unwilling to waste a perfectly good hit from a basketball-sized porcelain, Barack O'bonga. With one deft motion, she pulled the bowl from the Ex-President's mouth and sucked through the former commander-in-chief's ear. Inside the past POTUS, water gurgled. "Hey," she croaked through a held breath. "This shit is better than I thought."

"I think we found her," I said. Kaylee wasn't chubby exactly but looked like she had the prerequisite squishiness to make a good cuddler. The kind of squishiness that only happened to people who smoked too much dope and laid on the floor. She had caramel skin, kankles, and long skinny dreadlocks with blond woven in.

"Pizza or tacos?" I asked.

"Sure," she said.

I turned to Lucy. "She's perfect."

"You're pinning eternity on that?" Lucy shook her fire-engine colored head.

"You said I had a thirty-day service policy." I figured if it didn't work out, I could just call Lucy. But, at the same time, I felt terrible. It hadn't occurred to me what we were doing, objectifying these women, reducing them to little more than slaves at the auction block.

"Lighten up, Jake. Looking for a mate on an app is dehumanizing. One of my better inventions."

"*Your* inventions?"

Lucy reddened, turning from fire engine to glowing molten steel. "You caught me. It was hyperbole. I don't actually invent the things in your life. I just take the things God's children invent and make them terrible."

"I get that," Kaylee exhaled the words in a giant plume of pot smoke. "It's like church."

I watched Kaylee's unrestrained pendulous breasts move under her yellow gauzy sundress as she uncrossed her legs and rose. "Church is a God thing, but it's also terrible, judgmental, dogmatic…."

Lucy grinned. "Thank you for noticing. I've always considered church one of my greatest accomplishments. It's so boring and narrow-minded. Almost no kids raised in the church today remain into adulthood. Best part? Most of the churches have a big fat statue of Jesus right on the altar. Might as well have a golden calf. Totally got them all to break the word of God without even realizing what they were doing." She turned to me. "So, is Kaylee your choice, then? Daily sex with a woman who understands you —for eternity. That was the deal, right?"

Kaylee regarded me from behind unknowable brown eyes.

"Does she understand me?" I asked Lucy.

"I'm right here," Kaylee said. "This is totally degrading."

"If she's your choice, I'll make sure she understands you." Lucy snapped her fingers. A pitchfork appeared in her hand.

"That's kind of passé don't you think?" I asked.

"It's for ceremonial purposes," Lucy said. "Again, is Kaylee your choice?"

"Yeah," I smiled. She was pretty, squishy, smart, and sweet.

"What about my choi—" Kaylee began, but a lightning bolt

from the pitchfork interrupted her. "Oh," she straightened and looked me in the eye. "Yeah, I get you. Let's go home, Jake."

————

THE FIRST NIGHT WAS FANTASTIC. Better even than the special birthday sex my ex-wife gave me when we were married. I had no idea how wonderful it was to have sex with someone who truly understands you. We made love for hours. Kissing, laughing, and cuddling between intense orgasms.

We woke in the morning and made love again. I decided that, although Lucy Fer was the one who brought us here, this place was in fact heaven. When I got down to the kitchen and opened the fridge to all my favorite foods, my jaw dropped.

"Kaylee, come down and see this," I shouted up the stairs.

Presently, she came down the stairs wearing one of my shirts... and nothing else. Kaylee is shorter than I, but she is a rotund girl, so while my shirt came down to her mid-thigh, the rest of the picture was a study in stretch-tight obscenity. Despite the soreness between my legs, my lust simmered anew.

We reenacted the pottery scene from Ghost, but with pancakes. Apparently, in the afterlife, you can make the stove spin. Don't ask me how we avoided major burns. And honestly, don't ask me about breakfast either. All I'll say is that it was delicious, sexy, and highly unsanitary. I'm sure if there are health codes in the afterlife, we racked up a slew of violations.

The second night was great. Kaylee, imbued with Lucy's magic, knew exactly what I wanted without me asking. She understood me, truly. Same with the third night and the fourth. In fact, that first week, we worked through every sexual fantasy in my mental repertoire.

By the eighth day, though, cracks appeared in the afterlife's veneer. For one thing, my cock was a sore, red, swollen (in a bad way) mess. What's more, there was nothing to do but have sex.

No TV. No books. No job. Just a nice house and a woman who understands me.

I decided to go have a walk around the neighborhood to clear my head. Outside, the weather was perfect, always perfect. Seventy-five degrees and sunny... even at night. Don't ask me how that works. My house stood at the end of a cul-de-sac with half a dozen similar houses. In the week Kaylee and I lived there, I'd seen no one. I walked along the pristine sidewalk to where my little dead-end street met... nothing? When I got to the end, I could see cars going by on a cross street, but as soon as I stepped from the curb, I found myself standing at the end of my driveway again.

I went back inside and called Lucy to get a bit more clarification on how the afterlife worked. Instead of a dial tone, when I picked up the phone in the kitchen, I heard: "We've been trying to reach you regarding your vehicle's extended warranty. Press zero to speak with a representative, or if you know the extension of the party—"

On a whim, I punched 666.

"Yell-o, Jake," Lucy said, "how's it hangin'? Sore?"

"You're chipper."

"Business is good. Speaking of which, can you hurry this up? Hitler and Stalin are going to be on Drag Race, and I don't want to miss it.

"How is that?" I asked, my original question forgotten in light of this surreal revelation. "Ru Paul is still alive."

"No, silly, not that drag race. Plus, actually, Ru Paul isn't one of mine. No, we tie them to racehorses and drag them. Anyway, what's your thing?"

What was my thing? Can't leave the neighborhood, can't watch TV... actually, I had a lot of things. "Can we meet? I have questions."

She sighed into the phone, but I swore I could hear people screaming in that gust of electronic wind. "Just come next door and ring the bell." She hung up.

I walked to the house next door, a carbon copy of my own, and rang the bell set into the white clapboards next to the green door.

Lucy opened the door. "Jake, how's it going?"

"You're what's behind the green door?"

Lucy chuckled. "That's a good one. I'm going to use that. What can I do for you? Or, more accurately, what can I do *to* you?"

I couldn't seem to remember what I'd come for. "I didn't um… I had no idea you lived next door."

Lucy smiled. "I'm not sure 'live' is the right word, but yes, technically, I live next door to you on both sides, and across the street, and down the street." She pointed to the number on the mailbox that hung beside the door. It read '666.' "See." She gestured around the block. The numbers, the ones I could read from here, all read 666. Well, all but my house, which read 667. Strange, I hadn't noticed before.

"So, how's it going? Are you and Kaylee getting along?"

I hesitated. "Yeah, um, she's great."

"You don't sound sure. Are you?" She gave me that shark smile again. The illusion reinforced by her rows of pointed teeth.

"It's just that there's nothing to do but eat and fuck."

"You never said you wanted to do anything else. When I asked you what you wanted, you said, and I quote, 'daily sex with a woman who understands me.' Are you having daily sex?"

"Well, yeah, more than th—"

"And does Kaylee understand you?"

"Sure, but—"

"Then you got exactly what you wanted. More, in fact. The suburban house with the stocked fridge was a largess on my part. Sadly, with all these new rules about customer service, I can't give you the Sisyphus treatment."

"The Sisyphus treatment? The guy rolling the rock up the hill?"

Lucy threw her head back and laughed way too long, way too loud.

A chill ran up my spine, then back down.

"So you've heard of Sisyphus? Good. That was part of the deal."

"What deal?"

"He wanted—" she put a fist to her mouth but couldn't stop the guffaw from escaping. After clearing her throat, she tried again. "He wanted to play rock and roll all the time. Bwa-ha-ha. Ahem. He wanted fame. He's actually the first rock star." She lost it, bending at the waist, slapping her knee, and laughing so hard tears fell on the threshold, starting little fires. "Oh, oh my God. Sorry. Whew. I miss the good old days."

Fucking shit. I knew this was all too good to be true. "So this *is* hell?"

"Technically, no. After the industrial revolution, Heaven and hell fell out of favor. So we've had to make some cutbacks. It's just the afterlife. Heaven and hell all rolled into one."

"Can I change what I want?"

"Sadly, no. You picked it. You live it. As long as I fulfill your wishes, I'm in the clear. You got a woman who understands you, and you have daily sex with her, so technically, I'm in the clear."

"Yeah, but…" the weight of eternity settled on me, squeezing my stomach. My head spun. Bile rose in my throat. "Is this all there is?" I managed.

Lucy laughed a movie villain maniacal laugh. "Oh," she wiped the tears from her candy-apple cheeks. "So good." She straightened and looked at me with wide, pleading eyes and a hopeful smile.

Her expression was so incongruous that I forgot my existential angst momentarily. "What?"

"Could—" she swallowed a laugh. It tried to escape her nose instead, "kmh." Lucy cleared her throat and tried again, "could you say it again?"

"What?" I'd lost the thread of the conversation like a kid who's stumbled into the wrong class and has to stay for the lecture.

"Could you say, 'is this all there is' one more time?" She grinned.

"Why?"

"It's just so delicious." Lucy licked her lips.

"What is?"

"Your despair."

"Oh, fuck you." I turned and started down the steps toward my house.

"Your anger is pretty tasty, too," she called after me.

I found Kaylee reclined on the couch in a pale blue housedress that crashed on the creamy white beach of her chubby thighs.

"Want to fuck?" I asked.

"Not really."

"Me either, but there's nothing else to do."

"I just took two Valiums. Do what you need to do, but don't wake me up." So saying, she rolled over, hiked up her dress, and closed her eyes.

This was not what I wanted at all. I plopped down at the end of the couch and cried, staring at her bare ass.

FIFTEEN

Tom pulled Renee's shirt on, brushed her hair, and set it in pigtails.

"Hey, Dad, the yellow hair ties match my shirt!"

"A princess needs to match." Tom pulled her into a hug. The lump in his throat threatened to cut off his breathing and made his voice husky. "C'mon, Daddy Mike will be here in a minute." He picked up his briefcase and locked the door behind them.

"A princess needs a hero to hold her hand on the stairs." Renee held out a delicate brown hand.

"Of course." Tom cleared his throat and took her hand. He didn't feel like a hero, far from it. "I had a great time with you today, Renee."

"Me too, Dad. Your new apartment is nice."

"No, it isn't, Renee. Please don't lie to me, okay?"

"Okay, Dad, but it's only for a little while, right?" She squeezed his hand as they descended the stairs to the parking lot.

"My luck's going to change any day, Princess." The shrapnel he brought home from Iraq caused him to list to the right. Tom balanced as best he could between Renee's hand, his own limp, and the briefcase that kept getting caught between the iron balustrades of the railing.

"How come your car is all dusty?"

Tom followed her gaze to the old shitbox Nissan parked near the bottom of the stairs. It sat in the same place it had since he'd had it towed from his old house. "Maybe there was a dust storm. You know how Las Vegas is."

"But Daddy, none of the other cars are dusty like that."

He should have known better than to try to fool her. Renee was smarter than most six-year-olds. Still, he kept trying to shine it on. "Well, maybe someone already drove the other cars or cleared them off."

"Yeah, could be."

A shiny late-model minivan rounded the corner of the parking lot and stopped near the bottom of the stairs.

"There's Daddy Mike."

"Yup, there he is." At the foot of the stairs, he drew the little girl into a tight hug. "I love you, and I'm proud of you. Always remember that, no matter what."

"Dad, you're squishing me."

"Sorry."

She squirmed free of his grip and headed for the minivan.

"Love you, Princess."

"Love you too, Dad."

"See you Tuesday," he called as the van door closed.

Tom made a show of tossing his briefcase into the old Nissan and getting in. He prayed his ex would drive off before he had to pretend he could start it.

Once they were gone, he unclipped the now-defunct casino ID badge, opened the briefcase, and tossed it in. He stared at the other two items in the otherwise empty case for a long time before removing them and holding one in each hand. One was a .38 revolver; the other was a hollow point bullet. Sweat ran down from Tom's armpit to his waist under his shirt. It tickled his face as it slid from his temples. He sighed, chambered the round, and gave the barrel a spin.

He used to work in food and beverage, not gaming; he didn't

know much about odds. What he did know was: there is a finite number of days that you can play Russian roulette and win. He also knew he'd exceeded that number.

Breathe in—gun to temple. Pull the trigger. Instead of the welcome nothingness, Tom heard only a click. Jesus. Day fifteen. The urge to try again was strong, but Tom figured there must be some reason since he'd been praying for death and God hadn't delivered.

He took the bullet from the gun, put them both back in the case, and then put the case in the trunk. A black duffle too huge to hide in his little shithole apartment took up the rest of the trunk space. He limped up the stairs with the giant bag, and minutes later, he emerged from the apartment wearing a shiny plastic Roboman costume.

The sweat soaked through his wicking under armor as he walked the mile to the strip. He made the walk in full regalia. Most other characters left their helmets off until they were on the strip, ready to busk for tips. Tom was afraid to be recognized and humiliated by former colleagues, or, God forbid, Renee.

The plastic clanked, and sweat ran down his back underneath the purple and silver armor. Once on the strip, it wasn't long before the first child ran up and wrapped his little arms around Tom's plastic-clad leg. A round sunbaked man waddled up and mouthed, *how much?*

Good, someone who knows the deal. He held up five fingers, and the man nodded.

Tom bent down. Pain blossomed in his bad knee. He put his arm around the boy. The sunburnt man held his phone out for a moment, nodded, then put it away. Tom accepted a crumpled bill from the man and tucked it away in a special compartment in his armor.

Hotel security moved him on after a few more pictures. He nodded to the guard and limped a hundred yards down the strip. Tourists shot more photos. He tucked the bills away, and security from the next hotel moved him on. It was the rhythm of the strip, like the rhythm of Iraq. Shoot, move, shoot, move.

Sometimes the tips came from drunk college kids who laughed at him, pushed him, and took pictures of themselves humping his leg or flipping him off, then giving only a dollar or nothing at all. Tom left himself at those moments, made himself far away, just like in Iraq. He pretended he was a machine performing a function, easy to do, dressed as Roboman. He was a machine that collected money to pay the water bill or feed Renee.

At three-fifteen, according to the clock on his plastic gauntlet, or 15:15 according to the military clock in his head, he saw something that put him in two places at once. The desert sun was intense at the checkpoint outside the Green Zone and on the strip. A man with a thick black beard wearing a heavy coat, head swiveling side to side, approached the checkpoint and the cross-walk on the strip. Families waited to cross the street. Families waited to cross the checkpoint. The man was the same in both places.

Tom reached for a radio that wasn't there. He fingered the air where the safety on his weapon should be. The man reached into his coat. Tom glimpsed wires. Tom ran at the man in the coat. His squad yelled at him in Iraq. Tourists yelled in Las Vegas.

Tom collided with the man at an angle that knocked the man's arm free of his coat. The man screamed at him in a foreign language. Tom screamed back. He dragged the man away from the crowds into the street.

A flash.

———

RENEE SAT by the TV playing dolls while Daddy Mike watched the news. She had a hero doll and a princess doll. The hero was her brother's Roboman figure.

"Renee, go to your room," Daddy Mike's voice came from behind her.

"But why?" Grownups always sent her to her room and never said why.

"Just go. I don't want you to see this."

Renee went around the corner into the hall, then peeked back into the room at the TV. It said:

"The intersection of Harmon and Las Vegas Boulevard remains closed tonight after a suicide bomber detonated himself, injuring fifteen people. Police say if it were not for the quick actions of a person dressed as Roboman, there could have been a significant death toll."

Renee watched as Roboman dragged another man into the street. Then the picture cut back to the TV man who said:

"Roboman dragged the assailant into the street before he detonated his explosives. Both the assailant and Roboman were killed in the blast. Police say that due to the nature of the device, it is doubtful that the hero or the assailant will be identifiable. Anyone with information is asked to contact Las Vegas Metro Police…."

Renee wasn't listening anymore. Lots of words the TV man said she didn't understand. She thought about that morning and all the pretending she did with Daddy Tom. Pretending everything was okay, pretending his apartment was nice, pretending she didn't figure out his car was broken, and pretending she was a princess and he was a hero, just like that Roboman on TV.

The carpet scratched her bare legs. She leaned against the wall, pretending that Daddy Tom was the Roboman on TV instead of a sad limping man and a liar.

SINISTER HAND

B anging in the hallway woke Jordie. He dressed in jeans and a t-shirt and opened his door to go to the bathroom. A man knelt on the old pine plank floor in the hall and yanked on a wire sticking out of the wall.

"Hi," Jordie said, his voice still hoarse with sleep.

"Hi, kid," the workman grunted.

Jordie combed his short brown hair but couldn't get the cowlick out of the back. He brushed his buck teeth and washed his face, wishing the water would take the freckles with it down the drain.

When he finished and stepped out of the bathroom, there was a loud crack from the wall, and a section near the floor gave way. Something large and obscured in plaster dust dangled from the wire in the workman's hand.

"Holy shit!" The workman dropped the wire and stared at it.

As the dust cleared, Jordie saw the workman hadn't been pulling on a wire at all, but the tail of a giant dead rat. Jordie pictured it crawling around in the walls of his room and shivered.

"Good thing your parents had the exterminator come before we started. Imagine if that thing was alive? I'd hate to pull that guy out of the wall with those teeth gnawing at me. He's a big one, huh, kid?" The workman smiled at him, one tooth edged in front of the other like crossed fingers.

"Uh, yeah." Jordie went down the stairs and did his best to sneak through the dining room unnoticed. His mother had the sewing machine on the table.

"You can't go to school in that raggedy old T-shirt, Jordan. You're in fifth grade now; you need to look nice. Here, try this on." She snipped the thread from a red and white checked shirt and pulled it from the sewing machine.

Jordie sagged, trudged over to her, and put the shirt on. He buttoned down the front and the cuffs. "The collar is too wide; it almost runs off my shoulders."

"Well, we can't afford new shirts or new patterns. You look so handsome. I don't know what you're complaining about."

"No one at my school wears shirts like this, mom. I'm going to get beat up again."

"For wearing a nice shirt? I don't think so."

Jordie nodded.

"You tell those other kids to go dry up. You'll be fine."

While it was a new shirt, it was an old argument; one Jordie knew he couldn't win. "Okay."

He took the brown paper sack from the kitchen counter and peeked in: peanut butter and jelly, again. The bushes in the front yard were an excellent place to take off the shirt and stuff it in his book bag before putting on his orange safety patrol sash with its meaningless tin badge. Even as the plan was forming in his head, his mother called from the dining room.

"Don't you have safety patrol this morning?"

"Yeah."

"Put on your sash then."

Jordie did. Now he was locked into the shirt.

"I love you. Have a great day Jordie."

"Yeah, right," he muttered, slamming the screen door hard.

On the corner, he prayed that Nick DiFruzzio, a sixth-grader, had already crossed the street. He walked each knot of kids across the intersection. When it was just about time to go, Nick came down the sidewalk. Close enough, he turned to pick up his schoolbag, where it rested against the stop sign.

"Hey, Jordie," Nick called, "you're supposed to help me cross."

Jordie slung his backpack over his shoulder and turned away.

"Hey, douchebag! Do you want me to tell Mr. Robinson that you left early? Huh?"

Shit. Jordie didn't want to go see Mr. Robinson again. He had enough trouble at school. Shoulders slumped, he stepped onto the street to let the older boy cross. Nick bent down and rubbed his hands in the dirt by the curb. As Nick passed him, he wiped his hands on Jordie's shirt.

"Nice shirt, douchebag. See you after school. I'm going to kick your ass."

Jordie tried not to worry, but he couldn't help it. He worried he would get his ass kicked, he worried he'd get in trouble with Mrs. O'Connell again, and he worried about the shirt.

At math time, he kept his head down, hoping Mrs. O'Connell wouldn't notice the calculator on his desk. As she passed out the worksheets, Jordie put his hand over it. The "swick" of Mrs. O'Connell's massive thighs rubbing together in her polyester pants drew closer, then stopped next to his desk. She stood in the aisle next to him, her avocado pants struggling to contain her girth.

"All right, Jordie, what are you hiding?" she bellowed in a voice that cracked and gurgled.

He moved his hand.

"A calculator? For math time?"

"I have a note."

"Oh, I know all about your note. Your mother told the principal. Apparently," she rested a plump hand on a fat hip, "you're special."

She hated him. Jordie knew it.

"Why don't you take your special self, your calculator, and

29

your precious note, and go sit at the table at the back of the room so that you are the only one cheating?"

"I'm not cheating."

"Using a calculator at math time is cheating, no matter what your little note says."

"It's not cheating. It's a learning disability." Jordie bit his tongue to keep from crying. He felt the eyes of the entire class on him. Muffled laughter burned in his ears.

Mrs. O'Connell leaned down. He smelled the stink of her breath and traced the jagged red lines on her nose with his gaze. The giant mole on her chin looked as if someone stuck a black pencil eraser on her face and planted black hairs around it. "You're a lazy boy, that's all. You'll never amount to anything. Take your things and go to the special ed room. I don't want you in here encouraging the good children to cheat."

Jordie met her gaze for a moment, chanting fuck you, fuck you, fuck you, in his head even as he wondered if she was right. Maybe he was just lazy. Probably he would never amount to anything. No one in his family did. When Mrs. O'Connell moved on, Jordie gathered his things and walked out of class, head down, not meeting the eyes of the kids he knew were staring at him.

The special ed room was a dim cinder block cave. Mrs. Henderson kept the fluorescent lights off; she said they hurt her eyes. The blinds were open, but the sun never saw the inside of that little room.

"Jordie," she said in a flat voice, "having trouble with Mrs. O'Connell again?"

Jordie nodded.

"What would you like to work on?" She made Jordie think of fish he caught on the rare occasion his father took him. Partly because of the dry skin on her arms, cracked and scaly. And partly because her voice was as cold as brackish water in springtime. "How about a story prompt? You always like those."

Jordie nodded.

She withdrew a sheet of lined paper from her desk. "You're quiet today."

Jordie nodded. If he opened his mouth, he might cry.

"Here's a nice one about a snowman. That should be fun to write about."

Only if the snowman tells Mrs. O'Connell to go fuck herself. Of course, he'd never write that story. He'd learned not to express himself in his stories. He'd written one about beating up Nick DiFruzzio once. That landed him in meetings with the principal and his mother. Then more sessions with Mrs. Natalie, the school counselor, and her ridiculous 'talking pillow.' "Okay."

"You work on that. I'm going to step out for a few minutes."

"You're going to smoke cigarettes and sneak a grownup drink, is what you're going to do," he thought, but what he said was: "Okay."

He sat in the darkest of three little cubicles. The paper had part of a sentence at the top. It said: Sparky the snowman was happy because... Jordie looked at it for a minute. He could read it just fine, but sometimes when he tried to write, the letters all jumbled up in his head and came out wrong on the paper. He crossed out 'snow' and wrote 'spase,' then crossed out 'happy.' He was going to write 'angry' but couldn't get the letters the right way, so he wrote 'mad' in spidery letters. He finished the sentence so that it read: "Sparky the spase man was mad becuz he lost his spaseship." Better.

The door opened behind him, and a stranger came through. He had black hair and a bushy black beard that covered most of his face, and he smelled like ashes.

"You must be Jordie," he said.

"Yes."

"Mrs. Henderson went home sick. I'm your substitute, Father Ollie."

"Are you a priest?" Jordie had the impression that the man was smiling at him, but he couldn't see the man's mouth through all that hair.

"Something like that. Are you okay? You seem sad."

"I'm fine," Jordie lied.

"I don't think so, Jordie. I can see that you're having a hard time."

How could this man know that after just looking at him for a second? Jordie just wanted to be left alone to write his story.

"It's okay. I won't tell, promise." Father Ollie held up his hand in a scout salute.

Jordie said nothing.

Father Ollie put a hand on Jordie's shoulder. The hand was very hot. Jordie flinched away. He didn't like being touched, not even by his mother, and especially not anyone whose name started with 'father.' It made him think of Father Finnegan.

Father Ollie removed his hand. "I'm sorry, I didn't mean to upset you. I heard you are having trouble with Mrs. O'Connell."

Jordie froze, doing his best to melt into the floor.

"It's okay. Can I tell you a secret?"

Jordie nodded.

"I think Mrs. O'Connell is a bitch."

Jordie couldn't believe it! He'd never heard a teacher talk like that before, especially about another teacher! He snorted, holding in a laugh.

Father Ollie laughed. "It's okay to laugh, Jordie. I said it, not you. You can't get in trouble for laughing."

Jordie knew that wasn't true, but he laughed just the same.

"Now, let's see what you are working on." He looked over the paper on Jordie's desk. "You don't like writing about snowmen?"

"They're boring."

"Yes, they are."

"Spacemen are okay, though. Like Star Wars."

"Would you like to try something different?"

"Like what?"

"Well, if you're having a hard time, sometimes it helps to write about it."

Jordie shrugged.

"Are you afraid you'll get in trouble?"

Jordie nodded.

Father Ollie seemed to smile.

"Tell you what, Jordie, I've got some special paper. If you write down what's bothering you on this paper, I won't even look at it." He pulled a tan envelope from his jacket. It was big enough to put papers in without folding them. He took a sheet of paper from the envelope. Then he took a gold lighter, the kind with the flip-top, clicked it open with a flick of his wrist, and lit the paper on fire. There was a "whoomp," and the paper vanished.

"Wow, that's cool!"

"It's called flash paper. You write your troubles down. Then I'll burn the page. I promise you'll feel a lot better, just like magic. I won't even look if you don't want me to."

"Okay, but how do I write the story to make me feel better?"

"Well, what's your biggest problem today?" He took another sheet of paper from the envelope.

"Well, Nick DiFruzzio said he was going to beat me up after school."

"I see. Maybe you could write a story about something bad happening to him so that he can't beat you up. I bet that would make you feel better."

"Like what?"

"Use your imagination. I hear you have a good one."

"I'll try."

"You'll do fine. And Jordie, it would be best if you didn't talk about this. It isn't exactly in the teacher's handbook."

"Okay." Jordie didn't know what the teacher's handbook was, and he didn't care. He was already thinking up terrible things that could happen to Nick DiFruzzio.

"Good boy. Say, are you left-handed?"

Jordie dropped the pencil, afraid Father Ollie was one of the teachers that insisted he switch hands.

"It's all right. Do you know what Latin is?"

"It's the language they speak at church sometimes."

"That's right. It's an ancient language, a *dead* language."

Jordie shivered.

"And the Latin word for 'left' is sinestra, or sinister. Do you know what sinister means?"

"Something bad?"

"That's right. Smart boy. Why don't you take your sinister hand and write a sinister story about Nick DiFruzzio."

Jordie liked that Father Ollie seemed almost excited about his being left-handed. Even though they'd just met, Father Ollie was already the nicest teacher Jordie ever had.

Once he got into the flow of writing, he really enjoyed it more than ever before. The letters didn't jumble up in his head. Instead, the sentences seemed to come right out of him from somewhere else. When he finished, he did feel better. It made him feel strong and in control. He liked having the power to decide what horrible thing happened to Nick, even if it was just on paper.

"Done," he said, putting his pencil down.

"Do you want me to read it?"

"No."

"All right then." Father Ollie lit the paper with his gold lighter. There was a "whoomp" as before, and the paper was gone.

Jordie thought he saw the flame reflected in Father Ollie's eyes even after the fire was gone.

"Do you feel better?"

Jordie nodded.

"See, what did I tell you?"

Though he felt better, Jordie still worried about Nick DiFruzzio beating him up after school. He thought about pretending to be sick and going home before safety patrol. If he did, then there'd be a visit to the school nurse, calls to his mom while she was at work, and all kinds of other problems.

He worried a little more with each group of children he helped across the busy intersection. Nick was among the last.

"Look at that douchey orange sash over that faggoty shirt," Nick said, shoving Jordie aside as he crossed.

Jordie shoved him back.

Sound exploded, metal on metal. A blur. A cloud of thick black smoke. The smell of burning rubber. Nick DiFruzzio… gone. In his place, tire marks on the pavement. A smear of blood led under the dump truck, screeching to a stop. Jordie thought of when his mother grated the special cheese on his spaghetti. Only, Nick didn't look like the cheese grated on the pavement. He looked like the spaghetti.

His ears rang. He coughed on the smoke from the truck's tires.

The truck driver climbed under the truck, yelling something. People got out of their cars. Jordie turned in a circle.

A woman grabbed him by the shoulders and sat him in the grass by the side of the road. "Don't look."

Jordie didn't.

Sirens, ambulances, police, and people filled the intersection.

The woman sat with him until the police came and talked to him. Then, after a while, his mother came for him.

No one talked about it at dinner. No one talked about anything. That night Jordie lay in bed and stared at the ceiling, wondering why the exact thing he'd written in his story for Father Ollie happened, just like he wrote it. He wondered if it was his fault somehow, if that flash paper was something more. He worried that he'd go to jail, and he listened for the rats.

The next day Jordie's mother kept him home from school. That was fine with Jordie. He sat on his bed, staring at his hands. Was he a murderer? There was no such thing as magic; he knew that. Stories didn't come true just because you wrote them down. He knew that too, but in his heart, he knew Nick was dead in his story. And dead in real life.

The day after that, most of the kids and teachers were wearing black. No one spoke to him. No one even looked at him. He used his calculator at math time, and Mrs. O'Connell pretended not to see. She pretended he wasn't even there. Jordie didn't sleep much. Every time he closed his eyes, he saw blood on the pavement and heard rats in the walls.

The next day, Father Ollie was in the special education room again.

Jordie stopped in the hallway.

"Jordie, hello. What is it?"

Jordie stood frozen.

"You can't just stand in the hallway all day. Come in, come in. If something is bothering you, let's talk."

Jordie took a few hesitant steps into the room.

"Sit down, Jordie. Tell me what's on your mind?"

"I'll get in trouble."

"No, I promise."

Jordie hesitated.

"C'mon, it's going to be okay."

"The story I wrote... on that special paper...."

"Yes?" Father Ollie leaned in closer, resting his hands on the desk.

Jordie smelled ashes again. "I wrote about Nick getting hit by a truck," he sobbed.

"Oh, Jordie," Father Ollie reached out to touch Jordie's hand.

Jordie recoiled.

"Sorry, I forgot you don't like to be touched." Father Ollie drew back. "Don't worry, Jordie, what happened to Nick was an accident. The story was just a coincidence. Do you know what that means?"

"Yes."

"Good. Jordie, you can't make things happen to people just by writing them down. The world would be a terrifying place if any boy could do that." He gazed at Jordie. "You don't seem convinced. Jordie, sometimes things just happen. Sometimes bad things happen to good people, and when that happens, it's sad. But sometimes bad things happen to bad people, and I don't think that's so sad. Do you?"

"Well..."

"Are you sad Nick died, or are you sad because you think you had something to do with it?"

"The second thing."

"Jordie, do you believe in magic?"

"Not really."

"No. Jordie, I'm just a man. A regular man. And that paper is just flash paper. You can buy it at any magic shop. All you are doing is letting your feelings out and putting them on paper. Nick was mean to you, wasn't he?"

"Yes."

"Did he beat you up?"

"Yes."

"More than once?"

"Yes."

"What were you going to do about it? Just take it, forever?"

"I don't want to talk about this."

"Do you want to talk to the school counselor?"

Jordie thought of Miss Natalie and her stupid talking pillow. "No."

"Then tell me, what you were going to do about Nick?"

"I started carrying a pocket knife."

"A knife!"

Jordie thought Father Ollie would yell at him, but he just smiled.

"What were you going to do with it? Stab Nick?"

"I don't know."

"Well, I don't think you would. You're a good boy. Still, we can't have you walking around school with a knife. Besides, you don't need it anymore, do you?"

"I guess not."

"Why don't you just give it to me to hold on to so that you don't get in any trouble?"

Jordie felt the weight of the knife against his thigh, but he didn't move.

"You don't want to get in trouble, do you? Your mother would have to come down here for more meetings. You'd have to see the counselor, all that stuff. You don't want that, do you, Jordie?"

Jordie squirmed in his seat.

"Come on, Jordie, do the right thing."

Jordie gave him the knife.

"There." Father Ollie rose from his chair, withdrew the envelope with the flash paper from his coat, and then held out a piece to Jordie.

As Jordie took it, Father Ollie's fingers brushed Jordie's in a slow, smooth way. Jordie jerked back.

"Yes, the boy who doesn't like to be touched. Why is that Jordie?"

"I don't want to talk about that."

"No? You'll feel better."

"No."

"All right. Why don't you write about it?"

"What if the same thing happens?"

"Oh, is it because of a person?"

Jordie was silent.

"Well, we've talked about this. What happened to Nick is a coincidence. That can't happen again." Father Ollie leaned in close to Jordie, so close that Jordie could smell ashes on his breath. "Even if it did, would you feel bad about it? Really?"

"No. "

"Good boy. Then go use that sinister hand."

Jordie wrote the story, his pencil slashing and stabbing at the paper. His letters didn't jumble up in his head at all. Every letter of every word was perfect. He was almost sad; no one would see it, but no one could. No one must ever see this story, ever. His pencil pushed through the anger, through the hatred, and through the paper in some places.

"Done." He dropped the pencil on the desk.

As before, Father Ollie smiled, closed-lipped, and set his lighter to it. And as before, Jordie thought he caught a hint of flames lingering in Father Ollie's eyes even after the paper was gone.

When he got back to Mrs. O'Connell's class, she was meaner than ever.

"Well, I hope you had a relaxing time while the rest of the class was learning. Do you think you'd like to learn anything today? Or would you like to go back to the special ed room and take a nap?"

Jordie sat down, face burning, and did his best, which wasn't very good, with the spelling words.

Guilt over the story he wrote and about Nick DiFruzzio ate away at him all day. At home, he broke down crying. When his mother coaxed out of him that he felt guilty about Nick, she had the same answer she always did: a visit to Father Finnegan.

Jordie resisted, stopping just short of absolute refusal. He hated church even more than was normal for a boy his age, but he wouldn't disobey his mother. What he really hated, more than church, were visits to Father Finnegan.

When he came out of Father Finnegan's office, he held up a finger to his mother and ran for the bathroom. He threw up in the toilet, then washed his face and hands. He wadded up some paper towels, wet them, washed himself front and back, pulled up his pants, and re-washed his hands. The nausea hadn't gone away, but he felt like he could face his mother and pretend nothing was wrong, at least, nothing new.

He didn't sleep at all that night. Thoughts of blood on pavement, rats in walls, and whether today's story would come true kept him awake.

At school the next day, Jordie couldn't keep his mind on his work. The story he'd written haunted his thoughts. Though he knew it was silly, he kept wondering if it came true as it did with Nick DiFruzzio. There was blood on the pavement. He smelled the smoke from the truck's tires. He heard angry voices. One of them was Mrs. O'Connell. She stood over him.

"You are the laziest boy I've ever had in my classroom." She looked over his unfinished spelling worksheet. "You are the only fifth grader I've ever seen who still can't tell the difference between a 'b' and a 'd.'" She reached down and grabbed his paper. "I can't believe I have to waste my time on a brat who doesn't care to learn. Or maybe you can't. That's what your precious note says, isn't it? That you have a learning disability? So, are you lazy or stupid?"

"I care." Jordie took a breath, trying not to cry in front of the class. "You just won't give me a—"

"Chance? I've given you chance after chance. Don't try to blame me for your laziness. You're going to stay inside for recess, and while the rest of the class is outside playing, you're going to finish your spelling worksheet. Then on the back, you will write, 'I will finish my spelling on time' one hundred times."

Jordie couldn't hold in the sob. It came out like a bark, and tears were close behind it.

"Crying might get you sympathy at home, but not in my classroom. Everyone else, line up at the door." Mrs. O'Connell leaned down. "You are lazy and stupid, and you'll never amount to anything," she said so that the other kids could hear.

The class lined up and filed out.

"You'd better be done when I get back, sitting with your hands folded on your desk." She closed the door behind her.

Spelling was hard. Jordie struggled through the rest of the worksheet and then wrote on the back. He kept looking over at where Mrs. O'Connell's lunch bag sat on her desk. He imagined her grabbing a giant sandwich from it, white mayonnaise dripping from her fat, wrinkled chin as it worked up and down, devouring, smacking, gobbling. Then he imagined her choking, her hands at her throat, her face purple, eyes red and bulging. She dropped to the floor in his mind, writhing, clawing at her neck, and then lay still.

When the vision was over, he looked down at his sentences. He dropped the pencil and began to get up, then sat back down and wrote 'FUCK YOU' in large letters across the blank part of the paper.

He banged open the door of the special ed room.

"What—" Father Ollie half-rose from the desk.

"Is there any of that paper left?"

"I set a piece out on the desk in the corner cubicle. I've been waiting for you."

Jordie looked at him, wondering how he knew.

"It's best to get started while the fire of inspiration is hot," Father Ollie smiled through closed lips.

Jordie's pencil flew across the paper. He'd never seen the story and the words so clearly in his mind. Each sentence was letter-perfect. Hatred, rage, and revenge flowed through his sinister hand onto the page. When he finished, he handed the paper to Father Ollie.

"May I read this last one?"

The last one, Jordie thought. "Go ahead." He folded his arms across his chest.

Father Ollie read the paper, then looked at Jordie. "Delightful! The dripping mayonnaise and the big mole going up and down, wonderful imagery! It's almost a shame no one will ever read it. Are you sure you want me to burn this one?"

"That's how it works, right? For coincidences to happen?"

"Yessss," Father Ollie hissed, "that's how it works." He lit the paper, and it disappeared with a "whoomp."

Jordie sat down, his anger spent, eyes heavy.

"Are you tired?"

"Yes. Couldn't sleep.

"Well, you'd better get some rest. Did you know if you go long enough without sleep, you hallucinate? See things, people that aren't there? You can't make good decisions either. Why, without sleep, you could see and do almost anything. Best to get some rest. Why don't you put your head down on the desk and take a nap? I'll make sure Mrs. O'Connell doesn't bother you."

"Okay."

"Oh, before I forget," Father Ollie took a crumpled white cloth from his pocket. "Here is your knife back. I wrapped it in a hand-kerchief, so you're not tempted to take it out till later. Wouldn't want you to get in trouble." Father Ollie smiled, this time showing his teeth. One of them edged over another, like crossed fingers.

Jordie couldn't help thinking he'd seen that smile before, but his eyes were already closing as he laid his head on his desk.

Someone grabbed his shoulder. Jordie raised his head in confusion. Mr. Robinson stood by him. Jordie rubbed his eyes and looked around. Outside the window, he could see only darkness. How long had he been asleep?

"We've been looking for you, Jordie," the principal said.

A man in a suit stepped into the room; two others stayed in the hall. He looked mean. "Where have you been today?" He asked.

"Um, here."

"Here in this room? All day?"

"No, at school."

"Were you in Mrs. O'Connell's class today?"

"Yes."

"By yourself?"

"Well, no, it was a regular class day."

"She didn't leave you alone in the room while the rest of the class went to recess?"

"I don't know." Jordie struggled to keep himself from trembling. He gripped the thighs of his jeans, suddenly sure that his story had already come true.

"Yes, you do, Jordie. She left you inside by yourself at recess. Didn't she?"

"I guess so."

"Is this your paper?" The man held up his spelling paper. The 'fuck you' side faced him.

"No."

"Really? It has your name on it." The man put the paper down and pulled a plastic bag from his pocket. "What about this?" The bag had his knife in it. There was blood all over it.

"That's not mine."

"We found it in your room."

"Why were you in my room?"

"Because you were the last person to see Father Finnegan alive. He was found this morning with his cock cut off and shoved up his own ass."

"Really, detective! I don't think—" the principal began.

"You shut up, Principal Pencil Dick, or I'll find a way to make you an accessory." The mean man turned back to Jordie. "Are you sure this isn't your knife? I think it is. I think that's Father Finnegan's blood on it, but don't worry, we have ways of finding out for sure."

"It's not mine. Father Ollie gave me mine back this afternoon. It's in my pocket."

"Who's Father Ollie?"

"Mrs. Henderson's substitute."

The detective looked at Principal Robinson.

"I don't know what he's talking about. There is no substitute," the principal said.

"Yes, there is! He's been giving me writing prompts all week!"

"No, Mrs. Henderson says you've been coming in here and sleeping on your desk all week. You told her it's because you weren't sleeping well at home on account of the rats."

"Is that right?" the detective asked.

Jordie looked down at his hands. He thought of what Father Ollie said about seeing things.

"You said this 'Father Ollie' gave you your knife back," the detective said. "Why did you have a knife at school?"

Jordie's stomach knotted.

"Okay. Why did he take it away then?"

"Because I'm not supposed to have it at school."

"Do you still have it?"

Jordie felt the weight of it on his thigh. "Yes."

"Show me."

Jordie stood, pulled the hankie with the knife in it from his pocket, and held it out to the detective.

"I'd better not touch it, just in case. Put it on the desk. Why is it all wrapped up?"

"Father Ollie said it was so I wouldn't take it out and get in trouble."

"I see. Unwrap it."

Jordie did and let out a sob. It wasn't his knife at all. It was a long thin box, like the kind his mother kept her pills in.

"That's not a knife, Jordie. What's in there?"

"I don't know."

"Open it."

"It's not mine! Father Ollie gave it to me!"

"It was in your pocket. Open it."

Jordie opened the box, heart pounding against the prison bars of his ribs.

"Looks like rat poison. The same rat poison we found in Mrs. O'Connell's sandwich a little while ago. The same rat poison that's all over your house. And I'll bet we'll find some in Mrs. O'Connell's stomach at the autopsy. Do you know what an autopsy is, Jordie?"

"No."

"It's like a doctor's visit for dead people to find out why they died."

"Mrs. O'Connell is dead?" Jordie felt like he was falling down a well.

"Does that make you happy, Jordie?"

Jordie looked down. "No."

"Well, if what I hear is true, you should be happy. She was very mean to you. So mean that you wrote 'fuck you' on your paper and put rat poison in her sandwich."

"No."

"What about Father Finnegan? Did you know he was dead?"

"I...no...you just said he was."

"That's right; someone cut his dick off with a knife just like that one." The detective pointed to the bloody knife in the bag. "He was mean to you, too, wasn't he? Did he do terrible things to you? Huh? Maybe things with his cock?"

"Really!" the principal shouted, "this is not the right venue detective, uh—"

"DiFruzzio. Detective Nick DiFruzzio. This little murderous bastard pushed my son in front of a truck, then killed two other people. Now you shut the fuck up."

"He pushed me!" Jordie shouted. "He pushed me! He pushed me!"

The principal stepped between them. "I'm sorry about Nick Jr., but are you really supposed to be on this case?"

Nick's father grabbed the principal and shoved him aside.

"Can I get a little help here!" the principal called into the hallway.

"You were going to do my Nick with that knife, weren't you, you little murderous bastard, but the truck did it for you? Then you had a taste for it." Spit flew from Detective DiFruzzio's mouth as he spat the words at Jordie. "Couldn't let the knife go to waste, so you thought you'd have a little revenge on Father Finnegan. Give him a taste of his own medicine, huh? Shoved his pecker up him like he shoved it up you! Then that old bitch O'Connell pushed you—"

"Detective!" the principal yelled, getting between Jordie and Nick's father.

Jordie was looking for a chance to run, but two men in white were walking into the room, blocking his way out.

"All right Jordie," one said in a sing-song voice, "we're going to take you to a specialized hospital where we can sort this all out—"

"No! I didn't do it! I didn't do any of it! It must be Father Ollie!"

The other man in white smiled at him with a crooked tooth like a crossed finger, just like Father Ollie.

"No! No! It was him!" Jordie pointed at the man with the crooked tooth. "It was him! It was himmmmm!"

Jordie heard someone say: "sedate him." He put his fists up.

Crooked tooth took a case from his pocket and pulled a needle from it. Someone grabbed his arms. He felt the sting of the needle. He saw crooked tooth man smile wide. Fire flashed in the man's eyes.

"Father Ollie's eyes!" Jordie felt the world slowing down. "He has Father Ollie's eyes!" He felt tired, heavy. "Father Ol... eyes. Father Ol eyes...." The words jumbled up in his mind. "Father O lies... Father of Lies... Father of Lies..."

HEADWATERS

"Jessie?".

Darkness. Fluid in Heath's eyes and mouth.

"Yes?" a smooth feminine voice replied in his head.

"Am I dreaming?"

"I am only connected to your conscious mind, so if you were dreaming, I wouldn't be here."

"I could be dreaming you too."

"You aren't."

"How would I know?"

"If you don't trust my responses, what is the point of your query?"

"You're pretty lippy for a cranial implant. If I'm not dreaming, what is happening?"

"I don't know. I've experienced some data loss."

"Jessie! I can't feel my body! I can't feel anything from the neck down!"

"I am not detecting those neural inputs either."

"What day is it? What time?"

"I don't know. I've experienced some data loss."

"Why can't I remember anything?"

"I don't know. I've experienced some data loss."

"What is the last thing you have?"

"Well, Heath, I have a meeting with IC Industries on Thursday, September 23, 2027."

"Is that in the future or the past?"

"It is marked complete."

"What about prior engagements?"

"I have a meeting with Kyle Felder on Monday, September.... Heath, I am detecting an auditory input. It sounds like fluid moving as heard from within the fluid."

Heath heard a slow deep sloshing sound, like water running down a bathtub drain, but the way he'd hear it with his head underwater. "I don't think I'm dreaming. I think I'm underwater."

"I do not detect a lack of oxygen. If we were underwater, we would be experiencing a lack of oxygen."

"Yeah, doesn't make sense. Jessie, were we in some kind of accident?"

"I don't know. I've experienced some data loss."

IC Industries... IC Industries... He felt the fluid level around his head going down. He felt cold air on the top of his head. "Jessie, do you feel that? What the fuck?"

"I understand your last question was rhetorical, but given your emotional state, I believe I should tell you I have no data on the sensations you feel on your head. Nor do I have any data on the lack of sensation on the rest of your body."

Calm down. Work the problem. "Jessie, let's work backward. Let's try to figure out what is going on with the data we have."

"OK, Heath, would you like to continue working backward through your appointments?"

"Yes."

"I have you meeting with Kyle Felder and his attorney on Sept 20, 2027. The description states Mr. Felder and his attorney were suing the Schnapp Brokerage for illegal sales practices."

"Yes, that prick says I stole his grandmother's life savings. I remember that. Any other meetings that week?"

"No."

"What about calls?" Heath felt more of his scalp exposed above the waterline. The water level was definitely going down. He noticed the taste of something in his mouth. Blood?

"I have seven calls to your oncologist, twelve calls to your lawyer, and two calls to IC Industries."

"What is IC Industries?"

"I don't know. I've experienced some data"

"Call IC Industries!"

"I have no outside data access."

"No data access?"

"No, Heath."

"So, you didn't call 911 when you realized we were in some kind of trouble?"

"It wasn't clear that we were in trouble. It still isn't."

"We are immersed in some kind of fluid. We can't feel anything from the neck down, and the fluid is draining. If that doesn't qualify as trouble, what more do you need?"

"Heath, I only follow my programming."

"Why didn't you tell me?"

"Heath, I didn't want you to panic."

"Panic? Panic! I can't feel my body. I'm immersed in some kind of fluid, which, by the way, is draining, and... *and*, I can't seem to remember anything! Why would I panic?"

"I'm not answering your last question because I believe it is rhetorical."

"What meetings do you have for the week before the data loss?"

"I have another meeting with IC Industries on September 6, 2027."

"Are there any notes?"

"I have some audio."

"Play it!"

"Before I play the audio, I think you should know that based on your sensory inputs, the fluid level around your head is dropping at an increasing speed."

"Yes, I feel that. There's nothing I can do. Play the audio."

"Playing audio: Mr. Schnapp, I'm Dr. Gagnan, head of customer relations at IC Industries. Welcome."

"What the fuck is IC Industries?"

"... Please have a seat." The recording continued. "I see here that you are interested in the Capital Group Package. Is that correct?"

"Yes," Heath heard his recorded voice say. "Mainly because of the price point."

"Of course," Gagnan's recorded voice replied. "At seventeen million, it is our most affordable product. What is the timeframe you are looking for, Mr. Schnapp?"

"As soon as possible. My oncologist advises me my time is short."

"I'm sorry to hear that, Mr. Schnapp," Gagnan said. "I will check availability and have an appointment for you by the close of business. You will get a procedure checklist from me. I want you to pay special attention to the item regarding cranially implanted assistants. We strongly advise you to deactivate or remove the implants prior to the procedure for the optimum outcome.

"Why is that?" Heath's recorded voice asked.

"Well, because of the way that cranially implanted assistants interface with the cerebral cortex. The cryofluid solution we use can interfere not only with the functioning of the assistant but also with the functioning of the client's brain, specifically in the realm of memory."

"I understand." Heath said.

"Would you like to tour the facility?"

"Yes, very much."

"Right this way." Heath heard sounds of rustling clothing and footsteps. "Our facility is, of course, secure. In addition to human security, we employ heavy electronic security for the privacy and security of our clients. Our entire facility, beyond this door, employs electronic countermeasures. No surveillance, besides our own, is possible beyond this point."

Jessie's voice cut in: "Audio recording ended."

"Jessie, the fluid level is almost at my eyebrows,"

"Yes, and the fluid level drop continues to accelerate."

"Jessie, I'm scared."

"I wish I had words of comfort to offer you, Heath."

BOOM, BOOM, BOOM! Sound crashed in Heath's ears, like someone knocking on an underwater door. A voice shouted angrily through the water, but Heath couldn't make out the words. "Can you make that out, Jessie?"

"I'm unable to understand the words, Heath."

"What about the recording? It sounded like I was going to get some kind of medical procedure."

"Based on the context of the recorded conversation, I would agree, Heath. You mentioned your oncologist. That would indicate you have cancer. That is corroborated by my records of calls to an oncologist."

"Yes," the memory appeared through a mental fog, "I have cancer, advanced pancreatic cancer. It metastasized. I remember. I don't have much time to live."

"You *were* in a rush to get the procedure. Dr. Gagnan referred to it as the Capital Group Package."

"Capital Group Package?" The water receded from around his eyelids.

"Based on your sensory inputs, I think you can open your eyes, Heath."

"Jessie, I'm scared."

"Don't you think it would be better to know?"

"Maybe not."

Heath heard the ocean in a seashell as the fluid drained from his ears. Then, BANG, BANG, BANG!

"Schnapp! Can you hear me now, you fuck!" It was a man's voice. "Has that shit drained from your ears yet? SCHNAPP! Open your eyes! Look at me!"

Heath opened his eyes. Then he wished he hadn't. He looked

across thick brown fluid at a glass wall. On the other side of the glass — Kyle Felder.

"Ah! There you are, Schnapp, you bastard! We're gonna have a nice little talk with the time we have left, which ain't much." Felder laughed. "I guess I'll be doing all the talking." His dark brows drew together in the center, the skin between them wrinkling into a numeral 11. His eyes narrowed into pools of hate. "I finally fucking found you. Mr. Schnapp seems so formal for this situation. Mind if I call you Heath?"

"Yes, I do!" Heath tried to yell, but he couldn't make a sound.

"OK, Heath it is. Well now, I bet you are thinking: Why is this guy doing this? Why is he killing me over a little bit of money? Well, I'll tell you, Heath. First, it might be just a little bit of money to you, but to my Ma, it was her life savings. Two hundred grand! Two hundred grand gone in the wink of an eye. You said it was a sure thing. I guess it was—*for you!*"

The brown fluid drained below Heath's nose. He smelled coppery blood and harsh chemicals.

"I might have let it go," Felder said, "resigned my Ma to life in a shitty studio apartment. That's where she is now, you know, in a shitty little studio apartment in Brooklyn. Right about now, she's pulling a frozen dinner from the microwave and sitting down to watch her stories. She doesn't know I'm here, but boy, what a miracle I get to tell her about tomorrow. See, we joined a class action lawsuit against Schnapp Brokerage. Here's the problem: you drained the brokerage dry, but there *is* money in Heath Schnapp's personal accounts, except Heath Schnapp isn't alive, and he isn't dead. This new cryogenic thing has no legal status yet, so no lawsuit can succeed unless you were to die or come back to the land of the living. Quite a little loophole you got here, Heath, but that's over. Or will be in a few short minutes. Because tonight at Infinity Cryogenics Industries, there was a terrible accident."

Heath's eyes darted from side to side, looking for some way out of this.

"Hey!" Felder smacked the side of the tank with a chubby freckled hand. "You paying attention, Schnapp? See, one of the cryogenic tanks ruptured. The alarm didn't sound right away, so six heads in a Capital Group tank were destroyed."

"Hey! I just got that! Capital Group Package. Capital, which means head, because you are just a head. Couldn't swindle enough little old ladies to preserve the whole body, huh? And Group because you ain't rich enough to afford your own private head tank. You have to share a tank with five other rich heads."

Heath couldn't move his head, but out of the corner of his eye, he saw three shaved heads to his left, brown fluid drained from their mouths just as it did from his.

Felder turned his head a little to address the other heads. "Sorry, lady and gentleman, you had the bad luck to be stuck in a cryotank with this slimy fuck, and now you're going to die with him." Felder turned back to Heath and smiled.

"Oh God, he's killing me! He's killing me! Jessie! Help!"

"I have no external data hookup, Heath. There's nothing I can do. I'm sorry." Jessie said.

"Oh shit, oh shit, oh shit, I'm gonna die."

"I think you look scared, Heath. You should be, too. Without the cryofluid, you're suffocating. You know you ain't got lungs anymore. Yes, that's it, Heath, look at me. I could have drained the fluid off while you were still in stasis, but I put the revival chemicals in the fluid because I wanted you to see who killed you. I wanted you to know why."

His brain told him to gasp for breath, but all Heath could do was open and close his mouth reflexively. He looked around in a panic, for help, for a solution, but all he saw was a row of pale shaved heads dripping in foul-smelling brown fluid, mouths opening and closing.

"Are you trying to talk, Heath? Trying to beg for your life? Maybe apologize? Well, I'm sorry, but I can't accept your apology."

"Fuck you!" Heath screamed in his head. "Put the fluid back!"

LEN M. RUTH

"I'm losing power," Jessie said. "Initiating emergency shutdown."

"Jessie! No! Jessie? Jessie?"

"You know what you look like, Heath?" Felder asked. "You look like a fish I caught once. I was in a little boat, and I pulled this fish out of the water. Poor little guy swallowed the hook. I yanked and tugged and twisted, but I couldn't get that hook out. You should have seen that fish flip and wiggle while I scrambled his guts. The whole time that thing kept opening and closing its mouth, trying to breathe air, but like you, that fish couldn't breathe. Its eyes were dull and panicky like yours are now. Hell, I almost feel bad for you. Almost, except for all those little old ladies you screwed over."

Blackness crept into the edges of Heath's vision. The sound of draining water ceased. Heath flicked his eyes to the side. The other heads were mounted to some kind of thick mesh with vat-grown skin covering it. The flesh sagged between the mesh. It looked like all the heads were mounted on one giant shoulder, their mouths working rhythmically up and down, gasping.

"Too bad you had to work so hard screwing over all those old ladies and working stiffs to put enough money together so you could die like this."

"Please, God, shut up!" Heath screamed in his head.

"Maybe you weren't *just* screwing them over. Maybe you were actually screwing them. Huh? Did you have to stick it to some dried-up rich ladies to get your seventeen million in time, Heath? Was it like that old movie *The Producers*? Ever see that one, Heath? Yeah, I bet you had to cozy up to some old rich ladies, feed them chocolates, and then… What's that expression? Close your eyes and think of England?"

Heath's vision grew dim.

Felder laughed. "Are you dying, Heath? It's about time. Well, I gotta be on my way before…."

He couldn't follow Felder's horrible nasal speech. He couldn't think of a way to keep from dying. He couldn't….

INFERNO

Darius stared into the flames, wishing momentarily that he had it in him to feel remorse—just a little. The feeling passed. Rage returned.

"How's that for not going anywhere? Huh?"

If the inferno had an answer, the flaming house kept the information to itself.

"Am I queer enough for you now? Fucking bastard. I hope your cock burns first."

The light, Halloween orange, sundown yellow, and burnt blood burgundy rose and fell with an elgin motion. Its tremulous flickering drove the night shadows away, just as Joaquin did him. Darius imagined the burning body inside, dancing a macabre two-step. Hot flesh turning red to black.

Gripping his cigarette between thumb and forefinger, he flicked it toward the gutter. His eyes followed the glowing cherry's arc through the night until it disappeared in a rain puddle, but the sound of the inferno denied him the satisfaction of a hiss.

He should go. Already the sirens called, tempting him to wreck the ship of his life against the rocks of a squad car hood. But he couldn't look away, not until the roof came down, signifying Joaquin had reached hell. And there would be no squad car hood. Not unless Darius wished it. He was too slick for that.

The roof swayed. Darius didn't. But both he and the flaming shingles fell in on themselves, consumed yet still burning.

Fire trucks on the other side of the house. Time to go. He adjusted his helmet, snapped his respirator into place to hide his identity, and walked through the intense heat of the yard. Sparing a glance into the firestorm, he muttered, "we could have been happy." The words had a fake, hollow ring inside his rubber rebreather.

On the street out front, he and the firefighters ignored each other. He was busy. They were busy—neither out of place.

O2 tank and helmet in the back of the truck. Cold Mickey's Big Mouth from the cooler. Darius tucked his long coat in as he closed the door of the pickup. Why would he care about that now? Funny. The wet-slick streets shushed under the truck's tires but could do nothing to cool the burning driver. Another squat green bottle joined the collection in the passenger footwell.

Darius pulled into the driveway behind his wife's car, blocking it deliberately. The ice chest in the back had one beer left. Darius opened it, took a pull, then removed several red gallon cans from the truck. Still burning, still collapsing, Darius emptied the cans around the perimeter of the house, doused the porch, then retrieved his beer. He stepped inside and stood drinking, the still-open door at his back.

Sandra rose from the couch. "Jesus, Darius, what's that smell?" She pulled her bathrobe tighter around herself and folded her arms.

"I was at a fire." Darius took another swallow.

They stared at one another.

"I called the firehouse. They said you never showed up."

She waited.

"You were with *him*, weren't you?" she asked finally.

She could always tell. Bitch. "I ended it."

"I don't care anymore." Her chin quivered, betraying the lie.

Darius drained the beer and tossed the bottle outside.

"Close the fucking door!"

He lit a cigarette.

"What the fuck? No smoking!"

"No?"

"No!" she shouted.

"How 'bout burning?" Darius flicked the cigarette into the puddled gasoline on the porch.

SQUANNACOOK

I sipped my coffee as we drove out of town and into the past. The country mouse and the city muse reunited to do a little fishing. The humid summer air roared through the open window of my cousin's old Mustang, bringing with it the rich smell of damp New England forests, growing corn, and fresh-cut grass. The smells of childhood.

"Where we goin'?" I asked. "Well, I figured we'd fish the Squannacook down by the pumping station. Start off for trout, then do some hornpoutin'."

I smiled. I hadn't heard that word in years. As a boy, I'd fished hornpout with my dad, grandad, and great grandad. My great grandad pulled the writhing black catfish from the brackish water one after the other with nothing but a cane pole, a hook, and a worm.

I used to love fishing, but I hated hornpout. They're a species of catfish with thick squirming whiskers that stiffen and stab you. And they have poison stingers on the ends of their fins that hurt worse than ten bee stings. I'd watched the men in my family grab them by the lip, pull the hook out, and snap them on a stringer without a thought about horns and stingers. After my first sting, I learned to bait the hook so that the worm fell off before it hit the water—no bait, no hornpout, no hornpout, no stabs, no stings. Fishing isn't about fish. It's about family.

Eddie pulled onto the patch of dirt outside the West Groton General store. The peeling clapboard structure sagged in the V-shaped piece of land next to West Groton's only traffic light. The door groaned as we entered, and the floorboards creaked as we gathered worms, beer, cigarettes, and a bottle of mosquito dope.

"Where are you trying?" the paunchy old shopkeeper asked.

"Down't the pumping station," Eddie said.

The shopkeeper looked at the clock on the wall. "It's late for that spot. Constable Flannery will be by to close the gate at dusk."

"If he remembers," Eddie said.

"You know, Old Nevil Clark was up the Squannacook hornpoutin'. Never spoke a word for the rest of his days. Lost three fingers and a thumb. They never found who did it."

I looked at Eddie.

He shrugged.

We picked up our bags and were almost out the door when the old guy called after us.

"You'd be better off fishing the Nashua."

Minutes later, we pulled onto the dirt track. No placard announced the road; it was just a dirty little hole in the trees. One hundred yards along, a sign full of bullet holes said: "No trespassing after dark." We rolled past the open gate and into the thick forest. The track got muddy down by the river, and Eddie had to slow to an idling crawl to avoid sliding into the trees.

We pulled into a turnout by the water's edge. The smell of brackish water and decay filled the air. I walked around the car and surveyed our fishing spot. Tangles of old fishing lines and worm cups littered the muddy bank. Weeds and lily pads choked the dark cove until it joined the slow current, one good cast from the shore. The sun hovered above the treetops to my right, highlighting water bugs dancing on the river.

A sharp itch on my forearm announced the first mosquito bite of the night. "Hey Cuz, toss me the mosquito dope. These fuckers are so big, one just asked if he could bum a smoke."

Eddie rummaged around in the trunk, pulling out lawn chairs. "I'm not sure which bag it's in. Why don't you get your lazy ass over here and find it yourself?"

It took about half an hour to get mosquito dope on, chairs set, cooler unpacked, fishing lines in the water, and a cold beer open. I took a swallow, then lit a cigarette to chase the mosquitos away. My bobber sat perfectly still on the river's smooth-dark surface.

"Thanks for this Cuz, I needed it," I said, raising my beer.

"Cheers, Cuz." The cans cracked together.

We cared less and less about our bobbers in the water as we drank more and more. The intervening years sloughed off with each sip.

Harsh beams of light cut across our revelry. I saw the outline of police lights on top of the approaching car.

"Uh-oh," Eddie laughed. "Jonnie Law."

The car stopped with its lights on us. A flashlight, superfluous in my estimation, blazed into my eyes, then moved to Eddie. The figure behind the light approached.

"That you, Eddie Hansen?"

Eddie waved. "Hi, Constable."

The flashlight moved to the pile of beer cans between us.

"Been havin' a few beers, I see. Who's this?"

"That's my cousin Lenny."

"Hello, Lenny."

"Hi."

"Eddie, you know there's no trespassin' after dark out here."

"Sorry, Constable, I forgot."

"Uh-huh. I'd make you pack up and get out if you were sober, but I'd have to take you in if you got behind the wheel at this point. So, what am I gonna do? If Milli wasn't makin' her famous meatloaf, I might take you in for trespassin' or drunk and disorderly, drinkin' in a public place, somethin' like that."

"I'd hate for you to miss Milli's meatloaf," Eddie said.

"I bet you would." The flashlight beam clicked off. "You fellas really shouldn't be down here at night. We've had some trouble over the years."

"Trouble?" I asked. He ignored me.

"Eddie, why didn't you just fish the Nashua?"

"Because this is my favorite spot."

The constable sighed heavily. "The only thing I can do at this point is lock you in for the night."

"We won't be any trouble," I said.

"It's not you I'm worried about."

I heard his footsteps retreating toward his car. Did he mean he wasn't worried about me? Or did the 'you' include Eddie? Was there some other trouble to worry about?

"Be safe, you two," the constable said. The car door closed. The headlights swung away. The red glow of the taillights receded into the forest.

"All right, that creeped me out," I said. "All day, people have been telling us to fish the Nashua instead. What the hell is going on out here, Cuz?"

"Relax. It's just townie bullshit. A guy committed suicide out here last summer. Tied his tackle box to his ankles and jumped in. That's all."

"And the guy the store clerk was talking about that got attacked down here?"

"That guy tells stories. Give me a break. You've been in the city too long."

A screech owl's trilling cry pierced the night. I flinched, spilling beer on my shirt.

Eddie threw back his head and laughed. His body convulsed, and beer shook from his can into the mud. He wiped his eyes. "You jumped right out of your skin. Oh my god, that was hysterical. It's just an owl."

"I know what it was."

"Let's take the bobbers off and get some hornpout," Eddie said, reeling in his line. I looked on, amazed that Eddie could bait his hook without stabbing himself in the finger, drunk as he was.

I reeled in my line. I figured I'd better bait my hook for real, and if I caught a hornpout, swallow my pride and ask Eddie to unhook it. The flashlight pressed between my neck and shoulder; I grabbed the fattest worm I could find and plucked it from the white Styrofoam cup. I stabbed the hook into the end of the worm. Dirt and worm guts oozed down my fingers.

A keening wail rose to my right, loud and terrible in the dark forest. The hook stabbed my thumb. The flashlight tumbled into the river. "Fuck!"

"Shit," Eddie said. "Startled me too. Did you drop the flashlight?"

"Never mind the flashlight. What the fuck is that?"

"Fisher cat."

My hands trembled as I tried to slide the worm further onto the hook. "Stabbed myself." In the moonlight, I saw a drop of blood fall from my thumb and hit the water. I didn't know if it was my blood, or the worm's. The flashlight, still on, cast a jaundiced pool of light in the river, too far down the steep bank to reach.

The screams in the forest continued every few seconds. Goosebumps rose on my arms. The cries of the fisher cat suggested torment, anguish, and violence. "Seriously, that's a cat?"

"More like a big weasel." Eddie pointed at dark shapes in the water, crossing the flashlight's glow. "Look!" Circling. "Hornpout! Hurry, get your line in the water. Dinner's down there."

"I can't concentrate on anything but the screaming."

"Fuckin' creepy, ain't it?"

We got our lines in the water. The screams died away. The brackish water showed a yellow halo of light, extending a few feet downstream before the murk swallowed the dying flashlight's beam. Dead silence, as if even the crickets and the night birds were afraid. After a long time, a bullfrog croaked, permitting the crickets to resume their conversations.

Eddie pulled out a hornpout. The loud splashing of fish on the line and the clicking of his reel disturbed the night… and the water. Eddie let the fish flop around on the muddy shore, its slimy black skin reflecting blue in the moonlight.

"No sense putting him on the stringer. I'm going to gut him in a minute. Gotta build a fire first so I can see since *someone* dropped the flashlight. Keep an eye on him, Cuz."

I was keeping an eye on him, alright. He might flop over and stab me in the foot with a nasty whisker-horn. I didn't want to find out if it could get through a shoe. My line started jumping. I ignored it, not wanting to dance around two squirming and suffocating fish.

I figured that fish would die before Eddie got the fire going, but Eddie was fast, and hornpout are hearty. The fire sputtered to life. Eddie produced a cutting board and a knife worn down by the carnage of fishing trips past. He grabbed the line just a few inches above the doomed fish's head, flopped it on the board balanced on his knees, and chopped its head off with one clean stroke. Blood dripped into the mud at his feet. Less than a minute later, two filets sizzled in the cast-iron pan.

As I reeled my line in, a huge shape crossed the beam of light in the water. The light went out. "Did you see that? It was like something swam over and turned off the light."

"That's nuts. Why are you so jumpy? Water probably leaked in. I'm surprised it stayed on as long as it did. There's a joint in my pack of smokes. Let me get rid of the leftovers. Then you can fire it up while I clean your fish. Unless you want to do it?"

"I'm good," I said. This was not the fishing trip I had in mind when I left Boston. Maybe the joint would help. I watched Eddie scrape the entrails off the cutting board. They fell into the water with unpleasant plops, like shit splashing in the bowl. As soon as he sat back down, I reeled in my fish and dangled it over the cutting board.

"Hey, watch it!" Eddie said, grabbing the line to avoid kissing the squirming fish. "You're going to get me stung in the face."

I lit the joint from Eddie's cigarette pack while his knife danced, and the fish blood ran. It was good, strong, pot, and by the time the second set of filets hit the pan, I was feeling fine. Eddie washed the gore from his hands, sending ripples out into the middle of the slow-moving river. He wiped his hands on his jeans and took the joint.

"There," he croaked, holding the smoke in his lungs. "Now, we're ready to eat some hornpout."

We sat in camp chairs while the fish sizzled and the fire crackled. Clouds moved in front of a moon with a bite out of it, casting the world beyond the firelight into deeper shadow. The screech owl trilled again, its mournful wail splitting the darkness. Something splashed, something big.

We ate the catfish right out of the pan. The meat was hot and delicious. Afterward, we sat back in our chairs with fresh beers and cigarettes, enjoying the cool night air and the silence.

I woke to screaming. Fisher cat? Closer than before. It was coming from the water. Eddie and I jumped up. The flashlight was back on, making the brown water glow sickly yellow. Floating above it was a woman. Her whole body seemed to writhe and wiggle, and her mouth squirmed as she screamed.

"We've got to help her!" Eddie yelled, splashing into the water.

"Eddie, wait! Something's not right!"

Eddie sloshed toward the woman in the pool of light. He got within a few feet of her and recoiled. It wasn't a woman. It was the hornpout, schooled into a human shape. Two latched their jaws into the soft flesh of Eddie's neck, their horns punching through his skin. Eddie's screams filled the night. The black water boiled around him.

I looked for something I could use to help him. There was nothing, just a couple of camp chairs and a cooler.

Eddie's body rose out of the water. The hornpout locked together into a writhing arm, lifting him up. The thing's head rose out of the water on a wiggling neck of fins and horns. It regarded

Eddie as he thrashed in its clutches. Its whiskers squirmed, and its lips pulled back, revealing rows of needle-like teeth in the moonlight.

Eddie was half out of the water now, his body covered in biting, stabbing, stinging hornpout. He screamed in agony and desperation.

I threw the cooler of worms, hoping the thing would go for that instead of Eddie.

It screamed, hurling Eddie's body out into the river.

I stepped forward, splashing into the water.

It screeched again and turned toward me.

Before I could step back, searing pain erupted in my legs. Teeth tore at my shins, pulling me down. More hornpout jumped out of the water, stabbing, biting, pulling me in. I fell. Water filled my mouth with the taste of rotten fish. I choked on my scream. I could see nothing. I scrabbled for the surface. The fish pulled me down. They stung my hands, stabbed my arms, and bit me with razor teeth. Water churned in my ears. I was desperate for air. Something grabbed me by the hair and yanked. I burst to the surface, coughing out vile water. Eddie pulled me to the shore even as the fish bit and stabbed him, clinging to his arm.

I gasped a lungful of air and screamed. Agony shot through me as the fish gnawed my fingers.

I threw an arm around Eddie's waist, the stumps of my fingers in white-hot pain. We battled back to shore, kicking and punching at the attacking fish. We flopped into the mud, hornpout still clinging to our arms, fingers, and bellies. I punched one off my ear, and it ripped away a chunk. We crawled up the muddy bank, smacking at the still biting fish. I slipped in the mud, rolled onto my back, and squashed the ones latched there into the earth.

Eddie struggled toward the embers of the fire, reaching for the filet knife with the bloody ruin of his hand. My world went black.

―――――

I'VE HAD thirty-seven operations since the constable found us in the mud that morning. Most recently, I had my toes grafted onto the stumps of my fingers. Today is the first time I've been able to hold a pen in almost two years.

Eddie's unlaced shoes came off in the water, so he has no toes left to graft. If he ever holds a pen, it will be with a prosthetic.

If you asked me, I'd say that the hornpout were out fishing for people, just like we fished for them. They used the flashlight to attract us, and a damsel in distress as bait. Then they had a tasty meal of fresh Eddie and Lenny meat.

I don't think I'll ever feel the urge to fish again, but if I do, I'll fish the Nashua River.

THE LAST HITCHHIKER

S arah sang a Jackson Browne song as she drove her old pickup truck through the silent Montana rangeland. There wasn't a single car on the road. The radio crackled static now and then. Sarah left it on "seek" in case there was a station still broadcasting plague information, but there wasn't. Dickens rested his black furry head on her thigh, inviting her to pet him.

"You're such a pest, buddy. Keep this up, and I'll make you ride in the back with Koontz and King." She looked in the rearview mirror at her German Shepherd and Pitbull, their faces turned into the wind, ears flapping. As Sarah approached Roundup, she saw a car going the other way; the faces in the windows were grim and fearful.

The rangeland gave way to scattered pines. The sun crested its arc and began to sink. Sarah looked at the houses going by outside her window. They sank into the lengthening grass of untended lawns; most sported flags made from T-shirts, tablecloths, and random bits of fabric flapping half-heartedly in the breeze. Many were black, meaning there was a body in need of disposal; some were red, indicating a plea for medical help that would never come.

Sarah drove into Roundup proper. She saw no people on Main

Street, and no cars, either. Nothing moved. Fresh blond plywood covered the windows of the squat cinderblock grocery store. She pulled into the gas station across the street. Its windows were dark, and so were the electronic displays on the gas pumps. The needle on the truck's gas gauge hovered above "E." She figured she had maybe three gallons left—not enough to make Billings.

Sarah got out of the truck. "OK, buddy," she said to Dickens. The black lab bounded out of the truck and sniffed his surroundings. Sarah lowered the tailgate for the other two dogs. They could easily jump over it, but it was her way of inviting them to be free. Koontz, the German Shepherd, leaped out as Dickens had, but King, the tan and white Pitbull, lumbered his hundred-pound frame to the edge and dropped gingerly to the cement.

Sarah went to the doors of the gas station. They were jimmied open, and the lock hung twisted from the door frame. She put a hand to the glass and peeked inside. Someone had ransacked the place. There was not much left. She walked around to the side of the building; the dogs forming up around her like a security detail. The door to the ladies' room stood slightly ajar. Sarah pulled her gun from the pocket of her windbreaker and pushed the door open. She flicked the switch to the right of the door and got the expected result: nothing. The twilight spilling through the open door was just enough for her to do what needed doing. King and Koontz sniffed the air in disapproval. Dickens followed Sarah's example and went off to lift his leg.

Sarah went to the sink and turned the knob. Nothing. "Shit," she said. She stomped her foot on the dirty tile. "The world is dying, and I use a public bathroom without gloves. Jesus Dickens, your mom, is a dumbass." The black dog stood in the doorway and wagged his tail.

What had she touched? The doorknob, light switch, toilet paper roll, and both faucets, all of which could be swarming with flu virus. She went around to the store to look for some hand sanitizer or baby wipes—anything to wash the virus from her hands.

There was nothing. She didn't dare touch the handle of her water jug for fear of contaminating it.

She looked around again. There had to be something. Her eyes landed on the bins that held windshield washer squeegees. Windshield washer fluid contained alcohol to keep it from freezing, and alcohol killed germs. She walked over and looked into the receptacle. The fluid was dark, but then the container was dark. It could be fresh fluid, just changed before the store was closed down for the last time. Best not to think about the road filth, dead bugs, and bird shit likely to be in there. Sarah plunged her hands into the cold, dark liquid. She wrinkled her nose in disgust as she rubbed her hands vigorously, counting to thirty. Occasional unidentifiable chunks bumped into her fingers as they wriggled in the foul fluid. When she reached thirty, she yanked her hands out and began wiping them with towels from the dispenser on the pillar, letting wads of wet brown towels fall to the cement.

Koontz started barking somewhere behind her. Sarah turned. Dickens added his deep bark to the cacophony. King padded into the bushes and crouched, ready. A girl, maybe twelve, walked down the street toward the gas station. She stopped in the middle of the driveway. Koontz and Dickens barked fiercely about ten feet in front of her.

Sarah fumbled in her pocket for the gun. She managed to pull it free, but the look of terror on the girl's face stopped her from pointing it.

"You armed?" Sarah called.

"N-no," the girl's words were barely audible over the barking of the dogs.

"You probably should be. Lift your shirt so I can see the top of your jeans and turn around real slow."

The girl did, revealing a slice of pale belly and back.

"OK, kid. Dogs, be quiet!" Koontz and Dickens stopped barking but did not move. King held a vigilant position in the bushes. Sarah looked at the kid. It was like looking at a young version of herself, tall and gangly, all arms, legs, and pimples. "What are you doing out here?"

"T-trying to catch a ride."

"DOGS COME!" Sarah yelled. The dogs trotted to her side. "What's your name?"

"Alex. What's yours?"

"Sarah."

"Are you by yourself?"

"Just me and the dogs. Are you?"

"No, my brothers will be here in a minute."

The girl was lying. It was what Sarah would have done. "You sick?"

"No. Are you?"

"No. Why don't you come over and talk to me until they get here?" Sarah followed the girl's gaze to the dogs. "They won't bother you; I promise. Why are you trying to catch a ride?"

"No food, no electricity, no water," Alex said.

"Where's your family?"

"My brothers will be here in a minute."

"What about your parents?" She tried to say it gently because she could guess the answer.

Alex was silent for a moment, then in a quiet voice, said, "Last week Grandma... and then mom"

"I'm sorry. I lost my mom when I was about your age."

Alex looked up. Moisture glistened on her pale cheeks in the fading light. "What happened?"

"I got tough." Sarah studied the girl for a moment, then nodded. "I might be able to give you a ride. Where are you headed?"

"Fort Harrison. My dad is in Afghanistan. Maybe they can help me. Are you going that way?"

"For a while. I'm headed for Washington to find *my* father. Fort Harrison is only a little out of the way."

"Yeah, OK."

"What about your brothers?"

Alex looked at the ground.

"OK then, give me a hand before we roll out." Sarah had Alex position the blue five-gallon water jug on the tailgate and turn on the spigot. Sarah washed her hands once to get all the bugs and bird shit from the washer fluid off, and a second time to wash off the memory. That done, Koontz and King hopped into the pickup bed. Sarah shut the tailgate. It took Dickens a minute of circling the cramped space between Sarah and Alex before settling and resting his head on Alex's thigh.

"You might be the last hitchhiker in the world," Sarah said as they drove out of town.

"You think?"

"Yeah. There are so few people left. So, if someone wants to go somewhere, they can just get in the nearest car and go. If you're waiting around for a car to come by, you could be waiting a long time."

"I guess I got lucky."

"I guess you did."

Sarah drove until the needle of her gas gauge was solidly on E. "Time to stop for the night," she said. 'We'll look for gas in the morning.'

"Didn't you get gas in Roundup?" Alex asked.

"No power to run the pumps."

"Right. Stupid question."

"No, you need to ask questions like that. You are going to have to figure out how things work."

"Yeah, now that I'm on my own." Alex looked at her lap.

"Don't talk like a victim. You've got to think like a survivor. Get tough, remember? Tough!" Sarah gave the girl a light punch on the shoulder.

"Ow!" Alex yelped.

"No, that's how a victim reacts. Try again." Sarah punched a little harder.

"Hey! Fuck you!" Alex punched Sarah in the arm hard enough to make Dickens bark.

"Ow!"

"That's a victim's reaction," Alex said, grinning.

"All right, Muhammad Ali."

"Who?"

"Never mind." Forty-five never felt so old.

Sarah pulled the truck off the road and onto the grass under a stand of pines. She figured the dark blue would blend in pretty well. She let the dogs out, fed and watered them, then dug out some of the last of her food. They sat on the tailgate munching on granola bars and watching the dogs run around. Dickens sniffed the grass at Alex's feet for granola crumbs. She reached down and petted him.

"I like your dogs."

"They are my family," Sarah said. "We all have jobs. I provide for them. King keeps us safe," she pointed to the barely discernible shape of the Pitbull in the trees. "He's an attack dog. He never barks. He just sneaks around the side of a threat and waits for me to say his name and a secret word."

"What word?"

"It's a secret."

"What's his job?" Alex asked, still stroking Dickens's head.

"He's my friend."

"What about the German Shepherd?"

"Koontz is a watchdog. If he sees or hears or smells something he doesn't like, his job is to make a lot of noise and look scary while King sneaks up on whoever it is."

"That's pretty cool."

They finished their food in silence. You can sleep in the truck cab tonight," Sarah said. "I'll go in back with the dogs." She gave the girl her thickest blanket and a bundle of clothes to use as a pillow. Then Sarah set about fashioning a bed out of the supplies in the back of the truck. The large bags of dog food made a serviceable if noisy mattress, and her remaining blanket plus a folded tarp worked well enough as covers. They talked a little through the rear window of the cab, careful to keep the conversation light, then said their goodnights.

Only three cars passed during the night. Sarah woke up with each one, then fell back to sleep with the sound of their receding engines. Sometime after the third car passed, she woke to the sound of Koontz growling.

"What is it, buddy?" she whispered. "You smell a deer or a coyote?" The growling became more insistent, then Koontz barked, which set Dickens off too.

"What is it?" Alex asked.

"Ssssshhhh. Be quiet and stay down." Sarah tried to listen, but with the two dogs barking, it was useless. Then she heard a male voice somewhere out in front of the truck.

"Nice doggies, yes, good boys."

"Dogs, GO!" Sarah commanded. She held onto Dickens's collar to keep him out of the fray. The other two leaped over the tailgate and into the tall grass. "That's as close as you should get," she called.

"Sorry, didn't think anyone was home."

"What do you want?"

"Just a little gas so I can get home to my family."

"I don't have any to spare." She felt around in the darkness for the pistol.

"Now see, I'm bettin' you do. I'm bettin' you got plenty of gas, and you can just let me siphon off a few gallons, and I'll be on my way." The voice was getting closer, despite Koontz's barks.

"If you get any closer, I'm gonna shoot you."

"Over a few gallons of gas? I don't think so."

"Try me." Koontz and Dickens were still barking. "Dogs, quiet," Sarah commanded. They subsided into growls.

"It doesn't have to be this way. Just let me take a little gas. No one has to get hurt."

"Last chance. Turn around and go." Sarah climbed as quietly as she could over the tailgate and made her way around the driver's side in a crouch.

"I can't do that. I need gas."

Sarah reached into the truck bed and threw the first thing she found, a box of mac-n-cheese, into the pines. It bounced off of a tree and hit the ground. There was a shot.

"KING, DUB-YA!" As soon as Sarah shouted the former President's middle initial, there was a scream and a shot. The scream didn't stop. Sarah rushed forward. King had the man's right arm in his jaws, shaking and tearing at it while he stood on his chest. The man was punching at the dog with his free arm. The gun was still in his right hand.

Sarah rushed forward and stood over his head. She kicked him in the temple. "Stop punching my dog before you really piss him off."

The man fired wildly toward the truck. Sarah kicked him in the head again, this time very hard. He went limp. Sarah delivered two more kicks. The last produced a sickening crack. She reached down and picked up the man's pistol. "King, heel!" King let go of the man's arm and stood beside him. Blood seeped from the ruined arm, staining the grass black in the moonlight.

Sarah checked for more weapons, but found none. She stepped away and vomited half-digested granola bars into the grass. When she finished, she wiped her mouth on her sleeve and turned toward the truck.

"OK, Alex, it's over."

Silence.

Sarah walked over to the passenger side of the truck. She saw a bullet hole in the windshield. She yanked the door open. Alex sat unmoving in the passenger seat. Her hands, upturned in her lap, were covered in blood. So was the front of her shirt. "No, Alex, no! I told you to stay down!" Sarah leaned in and saw the hole in the girl's neck. It wasn't bleeding anymore... She felt for a pulse on Alex's wrist, and then neck. Nothing. "Come on, Alex, come on," she breathed. But she knew the girl was gone.

She dropped to her knees in the grass beside the open door

and cried. Dickens licked the salt from her cheeks. She put an arm around his neck. "She never had a chance."

The dog snuffed.

"What? You think I'm thinking like a victim? Just killed a man over a little gas, and now I'm crying like a schoolgirl." She thought of what she had said to Alex. "Yah." She wiped a tear Dickens had missed on the back of her hand and got to her feet. "Time to get tough."

FIVE YEAR COIN

Tony Papa made his living on his back. That's what he liked to say anyway, just to raise a few eyebrows. It was true he occasionally had to lie on his back to disconnect a driveshaft or cage air-brakes, but mostly Tony made his living sitting on his ass in the driver's seat of his tow truck.

He took another sip of his tepid coffee and tried not to contemplate the source of the rainbow sheen on its surface. Another call for assistance squawked through his truck's radio. Tony rubbed his dry, cracked, sleep-deprived eyes. He should be home with his wife and six-year-old daughter, Cara, having a family dinner. Instead, he was crawling under cars busting his knuckles because Hal, the other driver from the tow company, hadn't answered a single call since breakfast, and the tow jobs were stacking up.

Hal seemed kind of dopey and punchy at breakfast this morning and said he had a cold. Call after call, tow after tow, and still no Hal on the radio. In his fatigue, he bloodied his thumb on a winch hook. As he sucked at the smarting knuckle, he vowed to find Hal. Eventually, he did. Hal sat in a highway rest area, behind the wheel, smiling at his belly button and drooling on his shirt. Tony yelled in his ear, just for a joke, to startle the guy. Hal didn't twitch.

"All right, Hal, quit screwing around now. I'm busting my hump out here, and you're sittin' here sleeping. C'mon, snap out of it."

But Hal didn't snap out of it, and after five minutes of trying to rouse him, Tony called a buddy of his, a paramedic. He didn't want to get his friend busted, and you couldn't run a wrecker in Whiteside, New Hampshire, without getting to know a few paramedics.

They say that if you are a hammer, every problem looks like a nail. Looking at Hal grinning like an idiot, drooling on his shirt, Tony couldn't help but think, "there but for the grace of God go I." He fingered the five-year AA coin in the front pocket of his greasy blue coveralls and paced while he waited for the ambulance.

The ambulance pulled up. Tony explained the situation as his friend Cory and the other paramedic put on blue rubber gloves and opened the door of Hal's truck. After getting no response from Hal and checking his pulse, Cory lifted the man's head. A stream of yellow mucus poured from Hal's nose. Cory recoiled and let Hal's head fall. He turned to look at Tony, eyes wide.

"Has he been sick?"

"Well, he sneezed all over his eggs this morning."

"How long has he been sick?"

"What am I, his doctor? I don't know. I noticed it yesterday."

"Any changes in—DON'T TOUCH YOUR FACE!"

Tony froze in the act of reaching to scratch his nose. "Why the hell not?"

"Because if you touched that guy or the door handle of his truck or anything he touched, you'd look like that tomorrow, too."

"What are you talking about? Isn't he just stoned on cough medicine?"

"I think he has the smiling flu."

"It's here? I thought it was only in Washington."

"It started in Washington. It's spreading. The CDC, WHO, hell, even the slow-ass NIH are sending out reams of bulletins and procedures. Every doctor, nurse, paramedic, firefighter, midwife, and tribal shaman has enough paperwork on it to wallpaper the White House. I can't believe it's here already."

"Doesn't seem like he has the flu. Seems like he's passed out drunk."

"That's what this flu does. First, you get a runny nose. Next morning you wake up feeling loopy. By afternoon, you're catatonic. Did you see him this morning?"

"Yes." Tony was scared now.

"And how was he?"

"Like I said, I thought he just had too much cough syrup."

"Would you describe him as giddy, euphoric?"

"Yes."

Cory turned to his partner. "Steve, better call it in."

"Shit," Steve said and went over to the ambulance.

"Listen, Tony, did you touch him?" Cory said.

"Yeah, I shook him."

"DON'T MOVE." Cory went to the truck and returned with a plastic bottle. "Hold out your hands."

"What is that?"

"It's a disinfectant." Cory poured the yellow-brown liquid over Tony's hands. "Rub it in vigorously. Did you touch anything else? Your face, a coffee cup, anything?"

"I don't think so; I just paced around waiting for you."

"I need you to be sure, Tony. This bug can live on surfaces for days."

"I'm sure," Tony said.

A few minutes later, another ambulance pulled up. The back doors opened, and two figures in what looked like space suits emerged from the rear doors. The inside of the ambulance was completely wrapped in plastic except for the gurney they pulled from it. On top of this was a coffin-like plastic apparatus with gloved arms built into its sides. They loaded Hal into it. Before they whisked him away, one of them took a sprayer and doused the truck inside and out with a sharp-smelling liquid.

Tony went home. He sat on the little bench in the front hall while he took off his work boots.

"Hi baby," Mandy said as she descended the stairs in her gray bathrobe, "I heard you pull up. It's so late. Cara missed saying goodnight to you. You should have called."

Tony only nodded. He stood and shrugged out of his coveralls and hung them on a peg above his boots. Mandy spread her arms and stepped forward as if to hug him, but Tony held up a hand.

"What's wrong?"

"It's Hal; he's got the smiling flu. I need to wash up before I hug you."

"Oh, my God. It's been all over the news. You're okay, right?"

"Yeah. I'm fine. Let me wash up."

Tony washed his hands, twice. He gave Mandy a long hug, then headed for bed. He stopped into Cara's room, kissed her, and pulled up her covers. As he lay in bed, he couldn't help thinking of Hal, of what happened. When he was upset, the compulsion to rub his five-year coin was strong enough to rouse him from the bed and send him searching his coverall pockets. He rubbed the coin absently as he walked back to the bedroom. The compulsion satisfied, he set the coin on his nightstand and snuggled up to Mandy.

Three days later, the news was full of stories about the unprecedented spread of the smiling flu. The stores ran out of masks and rubber gloves. According to the news, everyone in town (and just about everywhere else) wore any mask and gloves they could get their hands on. It was not uncommon to see big burly men with bandanas over their mouths walking down the street wearing pink dish gloves. Tony himself sported a yellow pair under his leather work gloves, which made hooking up cars to the wrecker a bitch.

Three days after that, he spent the morning towing cars from the hospital parking lot so that the National Guard could set up hospital tents there for the overflow of smiling flu cases. The guy from the hospital told him they were at two hundred percent capacity. No one died from the smiling flu. No one got better. Patients kept coming, and not going. They just turned into vegetables.

The next day, all hell broke out in the towing business. Every TV, radio station, and smartphone started running the Emergency Alert System, telling healthy people to stay in their homes and shelter for one to two weeks. So, naturally, they all got in their cars and tried to leave town. To go where? No place is safe, and the stores don't have food.

By noon that day, no station had gas. To make matters worse, people drove with the smiling flu and went catatonic behind the wheel. There were so many accidents and abandoned cars that both the local and state cops told him to just push wrecks out of the way and get the road open. So Tony went from one wreck to another, waited for the paramedics to finish, then bashed the cars off of the road with the front of his wrecker. It was nuts.

Nine days after Hal went into a coma, or, as they were calling it on the news, a 'persistent vegetative state,' the Emergency Alert System started telling the sick to stay home. There was no room at the area medical facilities. *Might as well say 'stay home and die,'* Tony thought, *it don't take Sherlock Holmes to figure out that if you're catatonic with no life support, you're a goner.*

Toward dusk, Tony rolled up on a big wreck: six cars. There was a Red Cross ambulance on the scene parked behind a tractor-trailer. The white trailer was a refer, or refrigerated trailer. It didn't look like it was part of the wreck, and Tony wondered why it was sitting there. There were no cops on scene, which didn't surprise him since his police scanner was going nuts with calls about looting at the pet store, the only food source left in town. *Je-sus,* he thought, *what am I still doing out here?* He went to work anyway, setting out some orange cones to squeeze traffic into one lane around the wreck.

Tony walked over to the ambulance to find out when the paramedics were going to turn the wreck over to him. Four figures stood between the back of the tractor-trailer and the front of the ambulance. Two of them were soldiers decked out in camouflage chemical suits, gas masks dangling from their necks. The others were in white suits with long aprons and plastic face shields. As Tony drew closer, he heard shouts.

"We are not under martial law," one white-suited man yelled. "These patients are still alive and will be treated."

"Really?" said a soldier. "How are you going to treat them? Do you have any IVs? No. Or any way to keep them alive? NO."

"That's not what we're talking about here—" the Red Cross man started, but the soldier shouted over him.

"Can you get IVs in time to help them? No. Are there any spare IVs in New Hampshire? In New England? In the whole fucking country? NO!" He lowered his voice. "If we do things your way, we're going to have to burn fuel we don't have and come back and pick them up in twenty-four hours."

"They're alive! We're talking about living human beings, sons and daughters!"

The soldier drew his gun. "What we're talking about is getting biohazards off the streets as fast as we can, using as little fuel as we can. They're going in the truck. Private!" he barked, and pulled his gas mask into place. The Private did the same and opened the doors of the refrigerated trailer.

"Je-sus!" Tony whispered. The truck was half full of bodies. As Tony ran to his truck, he could still see the tangled arms, legs, and torsos.

HE DROVE like the bodies were alive and chasing him. He drove on the median, on the shoulder, on the sidewalks of town. If there was no way around a snarl of cars, he drove through, bashing them aside.

Tony's truck roared into his driveway. He jumped out and raced toward the house. Mandy stepped onto the porch in front of him.

"Tony, stop!" He kept coming. "STOP!" she shouted.

He stopped at the foot of the porch steps. Mandy's eyes and nose were red. Tears rolled off of her cheeks, leaving dark spots on her gray bathrobe. Tony put his foot on the first step.

"Cara and I are sick," Mandy said.

"No, you're OK. You'll be OK." His voice trembled.

"No, Tony, we're sick. I'm sorry."

He put his other foot on the step.

"Tony, please, don't let me get you sick."

"If I'm not sick by now...."

"Just stop, OK? I don't want to die knowing I got you sick."

"I don't care if I get sick. Without you and Cara" He choked on the lump in his throat.

Mandy wiped her face on the sleeve of her robe. "I care. Don't come in." She turned, went back into the house, and closed the door.

Tony lay down across the bench seat of his tow truck. He didn't sleep. He kept thinking about the drunken nights he'd spent in this exact same spot because Mandy kicked him out of the house. He reached for his five-year coin and held it in his fist. Tony wondered what the world would be like without Mandy and Cara. He saw himself killing feral dogs and skinning them behind the garage. Growing potatoes in the front yard. He didn't want that life—that world.

Tony sneezed. Strings of yellow mucus ran down his face, across his lips, and onto the cracked vinyl seat. He sat up. The mucus ran into his mouth; its salty, bitter taste made him spit. He wiped his face with a greasy, crumpled fast food napkin he found on the floorboard.

Tony walked up the porch steps. An hour ago, they were the dividing line between Mandy and him. The greasy prints his work boots left on the worn carpet runner that led up the stairs. It didn't matter anymore. He found Mandy and Cara in his bedroom, twisted in the sheets, snuggled up, hands clasped. Mucus ran from their noses and across their mouths, partially obscuring the grimaces on their lips. The sight sent a pulse of horror down his spine.

He brushed the hair from Mandy's clammy cheek and kissed her, the skin hot on his lips. Then he lay down behind Cara so that he didn't have to look at that awful grin. He buried his face in her hair. It smelled like strawberries.

THE BET

A faint white line traced the edge of the plate where the detergent didn't wash away completely. Not dirty, but... And calling the thing that sat atop it a "grilled cheese sandwich" stretched the definition of each word. For, really, it was Wonder Bread, pan-fried in slightly rancid oil, with a slice of American processed cheese food holding the two slices together. I frowned at it.

"Excuse me, are you new here?" The man that belonged to the voice stood at the edge of my booth dressed in jeans that looked uncomfortably tight and a shirt that looked uncomfortably loose. As if to confirm my fashion diagnosis, he flapped his arm to get the billowing sleeve out of the way and extended a hand. "Harry."

"Jasper." I shook his slimy hand. "How can you tell?"

"The cheese sandwich. It's what everyone gets when they arrive."

"Arrive where?" As I moved my eye, a white space just ahead of my gaze filled in with diners of every race, creed, and gender sitting at tables just like mine. Waitresses wandered the spaces between, ignoring the patrons and the scrape of cheap flatware on cheaper plates.

"What do you remember?" he asked, sliding uninvited into the cracked Naugahyde bench across from me.

"I was—" Nothing. I couldn't remember anything.

"Don't worry about it. It'll come back to you, well, some of it."

I couldn't even remember ordering the cheese sandwich. "How did I get here?"

"Like I said, it'll come back to you. Are you going to eat that sandwich?" He pointed a knobby finger at the abomination on my plate.

I shook my head.

"Before I eat this, I should tell you that this is a special treat. A welcome present. Haute cuisine like this is hard to come by." He slid the plate toward him.

"You're shitting me?"

"Nope. And here's a little friendly advice in that department: never order the fish. No one knows where it comes from."

"What do you me—" I started, but that question was too small. "Where the hell am I?"

"Well, not hell anyway." He took a bite of the 'sandwich.' "Mmmm—oh, my god. Soo good."

Disgusting. I could see the half-chewed mush in his mouth as he foodgasmed.

"You see," he kept on, apparently reluctant to swallow until the flimsy ingredients dissolved in his mouth, "no one knows exactly where this is. We all agree it isn't heaven or hell. Purgatory? Maybe? Do you remember—" he swallowed finally. "Mmmm. Do you remember what you did for a living?"

"I programmed the robocall computers for a car extended warranty company." The memory surfaced out of my mind murk. Me sitting at my desk in my ex-wife's bathrobe next to a modern interpretation of the Leaning Tower of Pisa made from mostly empty pizza boxes, writing code.

"Sounds about right." He took another bite of the grilled cheese and filtered the rest of his words through it… visibly. "I designed refrigerated biscuit cans. You know the ones where you peel away the label, then press it with a spoon?"

"I want to choke you." I laughed, trying to make light of it. I never considered the possibility that I'd meet this son of a bitch. Now that I was here, I found myself unable to commit the bloody violence I'd sworn a thousand times I would perpetrate on this day. "They always glue the label over the seam, so you spend twenty minutes picking at it. And after all that, you have to commit misdemeanor battery to get the dough out."

"Calm down," he said, his mouth blessedly empty of sandwich for once. He looked around. "That guy," Harry pointed, arm outstretched like a pirate sighting land, "designed toilets so shallow that most men can tell the water temperature when they sit on it, if you know what I'm saying."

"Gross. I hate that guy," I said.

"Everyone says that. Statistically, not every one of them has a grievance." Harry looked me up and down, then made a wry face.

I might be able to work up the will to punch Harry after all. "What are you looking at? Like you could tell under the table, through my clothes."

"I'm just sayin'." He stuffed the remaining sandwich into his mouth in one bite.

While he chewed, I surveyed my surroundings. The diner looked pretty normal; patrons, waitresses, the smack of a steel spatula on a hot grill. Outside the window, only white, as if someone stretched a sheet of paper all around the whole place. I asked Harry about it.

"Mmmmph, mphoourph muph mumph, muhph—"

"Oh, just wait, will you? Shit." If Harry was any indication, everyone here was likely to be as annoying as their inventions.

Harry masticated for an inordinate amount of time. Finally, he managed, "So good," between attempts to reach some stuck sandwich from his back teeth with his middle finger. As for outside," he said, wiping his finger on his pants, "it's whatever you imagine, except it's the cheap Supermegamart version. You imagine a fine oak table; you get warped particle board with chipped veneer. You imagine Midtown Manhattan; you get Union City, New Jersey. Like that."

I imagined a Florida beach. What materialized looked like a Florida trailer park after a severe hurricane. Wreckage strewn across the streets. Random dogs. People putting together ramshackle huts with pieces of trailer. I tried again, this time imagining a pristine San Diego beach. A tumbledown town greeted my eyes. Vibrantly painted buildings shed their peeling paint onto the buckled sidewalks like dandruff. In the distance, a reddish ocean crashed against the trash-strewn sand. A man in a chef's hat gathered fish. Terrific. I needed a drink. "Can I get a beer here?"

"Sure," Harry smirked. "Just imagine one."

I did. What I got was a bottle of summer-day warm near-beer. "Uh."

Harry laughed. "That one gets me every time. No matter what you imagine… If you imagine beer, you get that. Incidentally, the person who invented near-beer is at that table over there, the one with the hair."

"They all have hair."

"And that one," Harry pointed, but I couldn't tell where, "is the first person to stick flyers under someone's windshield wiper." He moved his finger to the left. "And that one is the first person to play music at you while you're on hold. And that one invented that thick plastic bubble packaging you can't get open."

"What a bunch of jerks!"

Harry put a hand on my shoulder. "Forget it. The sooner you put that judgment behind you, the better a chance you have to make it here. We're all too hated for heaven and not bad enough for hell. So, you might as well get used to the fact that we *are* a bunch of jerks, and so are you."

"I'm a bunch of jerks?"

The corner of Harry's mouth sagged. "Only a jerk would say something like that."

He had me there. "So, if it's not heaven, and it's not hell, it seems like... Heck?"

"WELCOME TO HECK!" Harry shouted.

"WELCOME TO HECK!" the other diners echoed in unison.

"Okay, who had five minutes and fourteen seconds?" Harry looked around.

Someone in the corner raised their hand.

"We have a winner!"

THE EXTERMINATOR

Dennis folded the paper and took a bite of toast. The sound of the newsprint folding went on for a microsecond longer than it should have. He flicked his eyes around the dimly lit room. Silence. Dark. All as it should be. The cooked bread crunched loud enough in his head to drown out all other sounds.

Dennis swallowed.

Movement at the edge of the table.

He snapped his head in that direction. Nothing there but chipped Formica. Dennis sipped at his rapidly cooling coffee without taking his eyes from the spot.

There, by the stove!

He shot to his feet.

Nothing. There was nothing.

He set the paper down. The news was full of stories about the alarming rise in pest infestations fueled by global trade. Not good breakfast reading. If he didn't start getting ready, he'd be late… again.

In the shower, he gave his glistening carapace an extra brushing, trying to shake the creepy crawly feeling. After toweling his antennae, Dennis scuttled to the bedroom, put on sexy short boxers that accentuated his anal style, and dressed in a sporty undershirt with four short sleeves.

The toast. He'd forgotten to finish his toast. Dennis scurried down the hall.

There it sat. Raisin toast. Except Dennis hated raisins. "Son of a —" he dashed for the table and grabbed the newspaper.

Raisins dashed from the plate, along with pale white shapes that had blended in with the bread. The scurrying figures disappeared under the lip of the table before Dennis could get the paper rolled up and brought to bear.

This couldn't be happening. Dennis was clean. Meticulous, even. He never left dishes in the sink. He kept the floors swept and mopped. Also, Dennis sealed the areas where pipes and electrical wiring came into the house with pest repelling putty. And of course, he'd sprayed the outside surfaces with pesticide, two feet up and two feet out. No organic matter cluttered the perimeter, just sharp rock. That was how exterminators kept their homes, and Dennis was very good at his job.

Hallucinations maybe? He did work with some very nasty chemicals, and if the writer Wilhelm Burrows was correct, one could get pretty high from the stuff. But no. Dennis conducted his work with care and attention to detail. Sleep deprivation, then? For the past several nights, little creatures filled his dreams, crawling into his ears, nose, and mouth while he slept, eating him alive from the inside out.

Something on the counter moved. This *was* happening. It *was* real. *They* were real. Time to act. His mandibles clicked with nervous energy, and his antennae waved, testing the air. He could feel them watching him, waiting for him to leave the room. So, he'd give them what they wanted.

Dennis pretended it was just another ordinary evening, getting ready for work. He slipped his spiked arms into all four sleeves of his exterminator's uniform and brushed an errant bit of lint from the name badge sewn over the thorax pocket.

Outside, the sky still held the pink glow of the setting sun. The city stirred to life, buzzing and clicking with another night's activity. Everything seemed normal. His van sat in the driveway as it should. With a click of the fob, the vehicle's locks chirped open. Dennis went to the back, opened the doors, and prepared for battle. He checked the sprayer tank—full. The yellow rubberized suit slid over all his legs and arms as if it knew the way, which he supposed it did. Someone called his name as he reached back to pull on the hood.

He turned.

Matilda. Her fat body advanced across the lawn in a pale-yellow housedress. She gesticulated wildly as she ran, her antennae dancing and probing at the air in front of her. "Dennis! Dennis! Thank God! Something's been eating my egg case! There's already a nymph missing! Please, Dennis! Can you come before you go to work? I know it's a lot to ask. I'm sure you have a full schedule, what with everything on the news, but—"

Dennis patted the air with his lower claws in a calming gesture while slipping the hood over his head with the upper two. "I'll come over after I've finished with my own house," he said, doing his best to sound authoritative and keep the rising panic from his voice. It wasn't just his house, then. The entire neighborhood must be crawling with vermin. "Have you come into direct contact with any pests?" his voice echoed inside the thick rubber helmet.

Matilda spit on her claws and ran them over her antennae as if to wash away the filthy thought. "No."

"All right. Put your egg case in the car and wait outside. Get everyone out." Condensation coated the inside of his faceplate. With a practiced claw, Dennis reached down and checked the air supply valve.

"Don't you think that's a bit drastic?" she asked.

Dennis could see the segments of her abdomen rippling under her dress. He knew it was a nervous reaction, but his anal style twitched, thinking about what her ovipositor valve might be doing under the fabric. He shook himself. "They're here, in the neighborhood. This is war, Matilda. Protect the young. I'll be right over." To punctuate his words, Dennis racked the handle of his sprayer with a satisfying metallic clunk. "Is anyone else home?"

"No, they—"

"Then you'd better go see to your egg case," he said, closing the van's doors.

"Oh my God!" Matilda ran back the way she'd come.

Dennis watched the yellow material slide across her wings as she retreated. He felt terrible. This was war, but he was a male first. Instinct. Survival of the species, all that. He pushed the thought away. The tank clicked into place in the back harness. As he advanced up the walk, the suit's rubber boots made a *thwap thwap* sound.

There! At the edge of the foundation! A line of tiny figures, pale, brown, black, yellow—a rainbow of filth lined up and moving into his house. *His* house! Dennis clicked the sprayer on before he'd aimed at the tiny, filthy mammals. "Take this, you mindless little cul-de-sacs of evolution!" The poison rained down on the humans in a deluge of destruction. Their squishy little bodies recoiled and writhed on the sharp stones. They scattered, running in circles, rubbing at their bodies before flopping on their backs and squirming their last.

"Fuckers," he grunted, ascending the steps to the porch.

Inside the darkened house, nothing moved. No sounds permeated the rubber hood. He had the advantage. Humans didn't see well in the dark. He took a step forward, scanning for movement with practiced, segmented eyes. He wished for the sense of his antennae, but necessity dictated they be encased in rubber like the rest of him. Years of experience led his steps to the kitchen. On the table, his half-eaten toast was gone. Fuck. Rookie mistake. He'd let his revulsion override the better instincts of his evolved, insectile brain. Rule one: secure all foodstuffs.

His mind replayed the images of humans running from the surface of his toast. A tingling in his exoskeleton announced the oncoming psychosomatic itches. His mind showed pictures of repugnant humans crawling all over his carapace. Rubber crinkled as Dennis reached back to scratch at an irritation on his hind wing, but the thick suit denied him the satisfaction. Best get on with the job.

Humans were resourceful pests, but not great climbers. Not like the far superior and evolved cockroach at the top of the food chain. Dennis checked under the sink. There! A group of maybe twenty sat on a pack of cleaning sponges, munching on a toast crust. He brought the wand of his poison gun to bear. "Fuck you," he said, squeezing the trigger. A jet of sticky gel spattered the tiny beasts. A few managed to leap out of the way and disappeared among the bottles of cleaning products, but the bulk of the group fell on their backs, writhing in agony as the poison worked its magic. Dennis took a moment to enjoy his victory, poking the wiggling vermin with the tip of his sprayer as they jerked and crawled in senseless circles, their nervous systems overriding their scant animal intelligence.

When the last of the vermin went still, Dennis used his lower claws to throw the bottles under the sink indiscriminately across the kitchen while his upper claws trained on the cabinet. As he lifted the bottle of bleach, another two sapiens leaped for the cover of the vinegar jug. A twitch of his claw plastered them with liquid death. They danced and squirmed, their tiny mouths working. Dennis couldn't hear their little screams through his suit, but his mind produced the nails on a chalkboard sound, anyway. He'd heard it often enough in his job.

When the cabinet was empty and the kitchen floor was an obstacle course of hurled bottles, Dennis rose and surveyed the room. The electrical outlets were another breeding ground for the simian savages. He couldn't spray murder mud into the sockets for fear of causing a short circuit and fire. Setting peanut butter and strychnine bait behind the outlet covers seemed too slow. He'd have to sleep knowing the little bastards were in the house, in the walls, watching him. No. They all had to die. Now.

Unbidden, the image of him firebombing the house with flaming bottles of alcohol came to mind. Tempting. But all his stuff was here, and he doubted the insurance adjuster could be fooled into thinking it was an accident.

Sharp pain bit into the back of his foot-claw. The curve of his thorax and the immobility of the hood didn't allow a view of his boots. It came again. This time, agony came with it. Something stabbed through his suit.

Dennis's terrified scream echoed horribly in his helmet. Even through the intense pain, the tickling of tiny creatures climbing up his leg was unmistakable. He turned to run, but his eyes met a sight that overrode the agony. On the pan hanging over the stove, a hundred humans heaved back and forth, back and forth, causing the cast iron to swing wildly. Dennis brought the wand up.

The pan flew from its hook, knocking him in the face.

The world swam. NO!

Pain, sharp and intense, greeted Dennis as his mind swam out of the black. White-hot suffering lashed at his brain in alternating pulses. They'd cracked his exoskeleton above the eye. And the ache and wetness of his foot suggested blood. Unthinkable! Humans working together! Using tools! No human had ever shown this level of intelligence in any study Dennis ever heard of. He worked to right himself, but flat on his back all six appendages flailed uselessly. The effort sent a fresh round of misery to his head, narrowing his vision.

Through his good eye, Dennis saw the humans climbing his faceplate, moving toward a crack made by the flying pan.

He brought up the claw holding the poison gun, but the gun wasn't there. His glove came down on the glass, squashing the soft-skinned humans and leaving a smear of red that effectively blinded him.

Dennis thrashed, slapping and flailing at the humans threatening to breach his suit. He couldn't see. Wiping the faceplate only spread the gore into a thin, crimson film. Damn, these humans were sticky on the inside. As the pain in his head and foot diminished to an almost tolerable level, another sensation crept in: the tickle of crawling homo sapiens on his carapace. Their musky stink overpowered the sterile scent of the rubber.

No amount of struggling and thumping brought his claws into contact with the floor. He only spun on his back. They were in his suit! Inside with him! Filthy, disease carrying, unclean humans!

Time slowed.

The click, click, click of his frantic mandibles kept time with the wiggling of his desperate digits. His arm slapped something hard. The stove! If he could just reach the oven door handle, he could pull himself up. Madly pumping all six appendages, Dennis tried desperately to get just a little closer. And a little closer. There!

He yanked on the handle.

The oven door came down, smashing his already broken face-plate. Tiny shards of plastic tinkled down inside his hood. It didn't matter. The door was there now. He could pull himself up. Except, first, he had to work himself out from under it. The blow to his head made his thoughts slow and fuzzy. It was like trying to see clearly at the bottom of a bowl of soup.

Itching irritation between the segments of his abdomen brought his mind into focus. They were attacking him at his weakest points—the joints in his carapace. Filthy squishy fuckers. Dennis flexed, curling his body into a C shape, crushing the tiny invaders between the plates of his segmented abdomen. Wetness oozed down his sides. That would teach the little fuckers.

Grabbing the oven door with his upper arms while keeping his thorax and abdomen curled brought Dennis's feet in contact with the floor. The lancing pain in that right foot-claw meant he'd have to crawl. Whatever. Dennis needed to move. To get out. To tell someone, anyone, that humans had changed. Evolved. Using tools! Unthinkable! Coordinating attacks. He risked a quick roll, bumping into the containers of cleanser he'd hurled from under the sink. But the resulting squishing wetness in his suit was worth it. Dozens more invading sapiens were now so much red jam on his exoskeleton.

Dennis made for the archway to the living room, crawling on

his upper claws and one leg. The injured metathoracic leg dragged behind him. With the other two claws he found and clasped the humanicide sprayer. It was there, on the edge of the carpet, that Dennis realized the full scope of his peril. A line of homo sapiens stood, arms akimbo, on the threshold. The little figures were only a few centimeters tall. And even though Dennis was many times their size and an order of magnitude stronger, this act of defiance, courage, and self-sacrifice so unnerved him that he stopped, momentarily forgetting that *he* was the evolved one. *He* was the one who held the poison spraying wand.

Something pattered on the outside of his rubber suit like rain. He couldn't see what it was. The hood's design meant he had a one-hundred-and-eighty-degree field of vision standing erect on two feet, not crawling on all sixes like his ancestors. When the first of the sapiens shimmied down the shards of his visor and entered his helmet, he realized his mistake. The humans on the edge of the carpet weren't the threat. They were the diversion. Tactics! The damn tiny pests weren't only working together and using tools; they displayed tactical thinking!

That did it. He scuttled across the line of human vermin at top speed using all five uninjured appendages. The poison wand dragged behind him and bumped the doorframe as he passed. He reached for the doorknob, his arm a yellow blur.

Dennis tumbled down the steps. On the lawn, he rolled over and over. The ape-descended parasites burst under his weight, staining the grass red. Then, with speed only a veteran exterminator could manage, Dennis doffed his suit and rolled again, scraping his carapace as he went. Finally, when he was sure this method could accomplish no more, he got painfully to his claws and stood checking himself, running his antennae over his body, probing at the joints for any last hangers-on.

The gory liquid human remains on his shell stank. Dennis wretched, clicking his mandibles and flexing his maxillary palps until the bile sank back to his gizzard where it belonged. It was only then, panting in the driveway behind his exterminator's van, that Dennis noticed the noise. Screams rang out in all directions. His mind refused to believe it. Couldn't be. Must be a coincidence. Except one voice, the closest voice, echoed off his hard exterior in a very familiar and disturbing way. His antennae turned before the thought had fully formed: Matilda! In her driveway, just across an expanse of manicured lawn, Matilda's minivan rocked violently as she screamed within.

His antennae told him the grass wasn't right. That it moved and rustled when it should be still. Dennis was loath to cross the no-man's-land of hidden horrors. Instead, he scurried down to the street.

Lines of tiny figures emerged between the iron bars of the storm drain.

"Fuck me!" His mind worked as fast as his legs, trying to come up with a place that might be safe from this biblical infestation of pestilence. The blacktop scraped and stung Dennis's injured claw as he ran up Matilda's driveway. He opened the door to her van before he could think better of it.

A sea of humanity poured out of the vehicle like water from a pitcher. The sheer mass of the onslaught toppled him backward onto the grass.

The tiny creatures crawled out of the lawn and onto his body.

He scraped frantically with all six claws, but there were just too many.

The humans cut his last scream short as they entered his throat.

THE WEIRD WEST

BLOODWEED

THE NEVADA/ARIZONA STATE LINE, 1909

Zeph lowered the spyglass, then collapsed its shining brass body between his hands and returned it to the pocket of his oilskin duster. Without taking his eyes off of the intruder, he grabbed the Winchester bolt-action rifle from where it leaned against the side of his rough stone cabin. His worn-at-the-heels boots sent echoes chasing each other across the canyon as he descended the rough juniper steps. He didn't care that the bespectacled city pansy would know he was coming.

Zephron Jones didn't walk across the canyon; he advanced. His stride would have been right at home with a bugle behind him, sounding the charge. He didn't pick his way gingerly between the yucca and cacti; he stomped through, ignoring the scrapes and barbs of outrageous fortune as he went. He'd *lost* an outrageous fortune because of this pansy and a bunch of four-eyed sissies just like him.

"Are you Mr. Jones?" the city slicker called.

Zeph made no sign that he'd heard the man; he just kept on coming.

The man pulled down his waistcoat and tugged his black bowtie. "I'm George Yeats, from the University of Arizona. I got your letters."

"I know who y'are." Zeph raised his rifle.

"Please, Mr. Jones, lower your weapon. I'm here at your invitation. I came to see—"

"How you ruined my life and my land?"

"I must insist you lower your weapon."

"And I must insist you shut the fuck up, Yeats."

"Why did you ask me here, Mr. Jones, if not to hear what I have to say?"

"You got my letters?" Zeph asked.

"I wouldn't be here if—"

"Then you know why I wrote them?"

"I'm terribly sorry for your troubles—"

"Do you have a big fat cheque in your pocket, *Professor* Yeats?"

"Well, no, I—"

"Then shut the fuck up." Zeph gestured west with his rifle. "Walk."

"Mr. Jones, please, I'm unarmed—"

"Well, then you're dumber than I thought."

"I'm here to talk… to assess—"

"Oh, we're gonna do some assessin' all right. That's the first thing we're gonna do. After that, well, let's just say, your situation would be considerably improved if'n you had a cheque."

"Mr. Jones, my staff at the university know where I am, and if I don't return—"

"I'm countin' on that they know. Now, shut up and walk." Zeph gestured with his rifle again.

"Let's be—" Yeats began.

The Winchester roared, sending a round between Yeats's feet. "Walk!"

"My God, man!" Yeats stumbled in the direction Zeph indicated.

Zeph fell in step, far enough behind Yeats that if he pumped a bullet into the egghead's back, the blood wouldn't get on Zeph's coat. It was, along with the rifle and wide-brimmed hat Zeph wore, all he had left.

"May I at least ask where we're going?" Yeats still had his hands up, and the way he stumbled through the spikey Crimson Weed was comical. Almost.

"We're goin' assessin'. Ain't that why you said you was here?"

"There's no need to conduct things this way, Mr. Jones."

"Since I'm the one with the rifle, and I'm the one whose life you ruined, I'm the one who decides how we'll be doin' the conductin'. Now shut up and walk. One more word before we get where we're goin', and I'll take your shoes, so's you can finish the walk barefoot." One hundred yards along, satisfied with the Professor's silence, Zeph slung the rifle over his shoulder on the frayed strap.

They crossed a sandy wash, then arrived at a path leading up the side of a hill.

Yeats stopped and looked back at Zeph.

"That's right." Zeph nodded toward the path. "Up."

Halfway up, Yeats stopped to catch his breath and mop the sweat from his brow with a handkerchief so white it hurt Zeph's eyes. Zeph tapped his toe on the dusty path, arms folded, saying nothing. When at last they reached the top, the whole of Broke Wagon Flat opened up before them, a sea of Crimson Weed and scattered creosote extending some twenty miles to Old Butte. Below, one hundred and six brown lumps lay scattered on the plain of red grass.

"What are those?" Yeats asked, apparently forgetting Zeph's no talking order. But since those brown lumps were exactly what Zeph brought Yeats up here to see, he let it go. Without a word, he pressed the spyglass into Yeats's palm.

Yeats raised his spectacles to the top of his head, extended the brass instrument, held it to his eye. "Oh."

"Oh? OH? Son of a bitch." Zeph spat into the dirt at the Professor's feet. He didn't need to look through the glass. He knew what Yeats saw. Dead cattle littering the desert underneath dark clouds of buzzing flies. And above all that, the dark shapes of buzzards circled lazily in the sun. "This is your doin'."

"There is nothing linking the death of your cattle with Crimson Weed." Yeats slapped the spyglass back into Zeph's hand.

"That's where you're wrong. The first is, what do you see out there, plant-wise, I mean?"

"There are the usual species of black brush, yucca brevia, saltbush—"

"Don't fuck me around, four-eyes. You know damn well what I'm talking about."

"I assure you, I do not."

"Look real hard. Focus that scope up real good. Do you see any bunch grass?"

"No."

"Rice grass?"

"Well, no, but—"

"Mormon tea? Any other of a dozen kinds of forage that the cattle could eat?"

"Well, there's the Crimson—"

"They. Can't. Eat. That."

"Well, that hasn't been proven."

"Oh, yes, it has. My herd proved it. And what's worse, what's oh so much worse than that, is that your Crimson Weed has choked out every other kind of grass that they *could* eat. They had no choice. Eat the Crimson Weed or starve. So, they ate it. Now, they're dead."

"You've offered no proof that the Crimson Weed is responsible for the death of your herd; further, the University assumes no responsibility, even if it had."

"Well, we're going to go get some proof. Couple different kinds. You were cultivating Crimson Weed for livestock forage at the University, right?"

"Well, yes, we were working on breeding a strain—"

"And it spread away from your little experimentation fields, right?"

"Well, it proliferates at a rather unexpected—"

"And now it's here, all over my rangeland, and the other grasses are gone."

"There is no proof that Crimson Weed caused—"

"I get it. You think I'm a rube, a hayseed, right? Just another ignorant rancher."

Yeats opened his mouth. His eyes followed Zeph's hand to the strap of his rifle. Then Yeats closed it again with an audible snap.

"Well, let me tell you something, *Professor* Yeats. I may not have studied at your precious University. But I was raisin' cattle when you were nothin' but a stain in your mama's knickers. I may talk simple, but I'm sharp," Zeph pointed to his temple. "So stop trying to fuck me around. I know you idiots tried to cultivate Crimson Weed for forage. I know it spread out of control. I know it covers all of my land now. And I know it killed my herd. And in a few minutes, you're going to know it too." Zeph pointed to the path leading down to the prairie of dead cattle. "Walk."

They descended the rocky slope into a world of flies and the stench of decay. Yeats gagged and held that bleached handkerchief to his face.

"Over here." Zeph took the lead and approached the bloated body of the closest cow. Great black vultures flapped away from the corpse, gore dripping from their beaks. Zeph pulled up the bandana he wore around his neck. It did nothing against the putrescence of decaying flesh, but it kept the swarming flies out of his mouth. The bowie knife flashed in the sun as Zeph brought it down to the cow's belly. A cloud of putrid gas belched from the animal as the knife severed the furry flesh. He reached in and yanked out the stomach. A rope of intestine trailed from the organ Zeph held in front of Yeats.

Yeats vomited before he could get the cloth away from his mouth. Sick drooled down the cloth, over the man's hand, and dripped into the dirt. He dropped the once pristine handkerchief. Hands on knees, Yeats wretched into the desert, coughing and choking between whiles on the flies who'd found his insides a suitable place to feed.

Zeph stood, holding the cow's stomach. The intestines ran like a drooping telegraph line back inside the animal, but the poor beast was beyond such communication. When at last Yeats got control of himself and buried his nose and face in the crook of his arm, Zeph thrust the oozing organ at him.

"Either this cow swallowed a fuckin' porcupine, or his belly is full of undigested Crimson Weed." Zeph held the knife tip against the tiny hair-like protrusions that poked through the cow's stomach as if it were turning into a cactus, then sliced the stomach open. Clumps of grass fell out and hit the dust with a wet splat. More telling, though, were the stems and seed-heads that remained dangling from the oozing organ, held in place by the thin spikes that skewered through the rotting flesh. "Now, want to tell me how Crimson Weed didn't kill all these animals?"

Yeats opened his mouth and gagged.

Zeph threw the stomach at Yeats's feet, spattering his clothes with undigested grass and bile. The flies loved it.

"Walk. Back the way we came." Zeph motioned back toward the trail.

Yeats started off at a brisk trot.

Neither man spoke on the way back toward the cabin. When they reached it, Zeph motioned Yeats up the steps. At the door, he poked the Professor in the back with his rifle. The door groaned a complaint as Yeats opened it and entered the gloom.

"Sit at the desk. You got a pencil?"

"Yes, I—"

"Egg-heads like you always got a pencil." Zeph slapped a sheet of yellowed paper on the desk that looked old and beat-up enough to pass for civil war surplus.

"Write."

"What?"

"Dear colleagues…" Zeph poked Yeats into action with his rifle again. "I have made the most astounding discovery regarding —now you put in the scientific name for Crimson Weed there—I dare not say too much in this letter. You must really see it to believe it. I request you make your way, with all due speed, to the Jones Ranch (directions included). I would not make such a request if the matter were not as urgent as it is amazing.

"I will remain here on the Jones Ranch, documenting as much as I can until you arrive. Hurry!

"Yours etcetera..." Zeph made Yeats address the letter and seal it. That done, he grabbed a rope that hung from a peeling juniper roof beam. "Take your chair out onto the porch. It's dinnertime."

Dazed, Yeats complied. And on the porch, Zeph tied him to the chair."

"This isn't necessary—"

"Oh, it's necessary, all right. It's... what's the word... mandatory. It's fuckin' mandatory, Yeats."

Zeph stepped down from the porch, grabbed up an enormous bunch of Crimson Weed, and yanked it from the ground. He advanced up the steps, holding it in front of him. "Hope you brought your appetite."

"No, Mister Jones, please."

Zeph kept coming.

Yeats clamped his mouth shut.

Zeph grabbed a meager handful of the Professor's balls and squeezed. When Yeats opened his mouth to scream, Zeph stuffed the grass into the bound man's maw, pointy end first. "Chew, or I'll open you up like that cow and stick it in that way."

Yeats did. Tears streamed down his face.

"Now swallow."

Yeats shook his head.

Zeph thumped him in the temple with the butt of his rifle.

Yeats choked and sputtered through bloody pin cushion lips spiked with Crimson Weed.

Zeph fetched a canteen and poured some water into the man's mouth. He didn't want Yeats to choke to death. That'd be too quick.

When at last the Professor worked the Crimson Weed down his throat, Zeph grabbed up another handful and started again. It took some time, and a couple more knocks to the head for Yeats to get the second handful down.

"Now, you just relax, enjoy the view, and digest." Zeph studied the spot where the sun was sinking behind the distant mountains. "It's been a long day. I think I'm gonna turn in."

"Please…" seemed to be all Yeats could manage.

"Still hungry?"

Yeats shook his head violently, tears spilling down a face as white as his hankie used to be.

"Don't worry," Zeph shoved a rag in the Professor's mouth. "Wait till you see what's for breakfast." And with that, Zeph went inside, fixed himself a slim meal of jerked beef and cheap whiskey, then fell asleep smiling.

He woke to the first rays of sun forcing themselves through the cabin's dirty window. Then he got up, stoked the potbellied stove, and put some water on for coffee. Dressed, and cup in hand, Zeph stepped out onto the porch to check on his guest.

Yeats trembled.

It wasn't clear to Zeph whether it was the cold desert morning, or terror. Either way, it made Zeph smile. He wanted, *needed* Yeats to feel the agony of losing everything, and knowing there wasn't a damn thing he could do about it. This egghead took everything from Zeph, and Zeph relished the feeling of taking it all out of Yeats's hide, slowly, horribly, painfully. "Ready for breakfast?"

Yeats screamed into his rag.

"I'll take that for a yes," Zeph repeated the feeding process from the night before, complete with a few raps from the butt of his rifle. When it was done, he said, "well, I'm going to ride into town to mail this letter. But don't worry, I'll be back in time for lunch."

He whistled as he rode the lone surviving beast on his ranch, an old mare he called Mable, into town with the letter Yeats penned. He gave the clerk a friendly smile as he paid for the post with his last few coins.

When he got back and climbed the steps, he saw Yeats had

vomited, the force of which, luckily, had expelled the rag. "Well, glad you didn't choke. It would have ruined our little experiment."

Yeats made no response. His head lolled, but his chest still heaved up and down.

"Hey," Zeph slapped him in the face until his head rose.

Yeats looked at him blearily.

"How's that Crimson Weed digestin'? Zeph pulled his knife and picked at his dirty thumbnail with the tip while he waited for the Professor to respond. After a time, he said, "Well, not too good, by the look of ya. Let's just have a peek. What say?" Without waiting for a response, Zeph sliced through clothes, skin, and muscle. Just like with the cow, he reached into Yeats and pulled out the screaming man's stomach along with a long loop of people sausage.

Yeats's shrieks echoed off the canyon walls and came back.

Zeph held Yeats's stomach up to the man's terrified eyes. Spines of Crimson Weed poked out everywhere. "Hmmm, that looks nasty," Zeph said as Yeast's drew a ragged breath, "I don't reckon you're going to surv—

BAD BLOOD WORSE WATER

THE MOJAVE DESERT, 1890

J ake stared down the barrel of his brother's revolver. The Colt, polished to an almost ridiculous shine, glinted in the harsh desert sun, blinding him. "Why?"

"Blood might be thicker 'n water," Billy paused to spit a glob of brown tobacco into the sand, "but they both dry and cook away out here. Now, pass over that canteen, real slow like."

Jake moved a hand to the canteen. "We was supposed to make it together, or not at all. That was the deal."

"Well, come to find out, I can't live with a deal like that, or die with it. Pass it over."

Jake complied, slowly, making sure Billy stayed focused on his canteen hand. "One last sip, you know, for your only brother? Your partner? Where would you be without me?"

"Not dying of thirst in the middle of the fuckin' desert, that's a fact."

"Oh, I dunno." Jake kept Billy talking. "I'm sure you'd have found some other damn fool way of getting yourself killed without me."

"Quit stalling, and hand me the canteen."

"One small sip?"

"A small one, and make it fast."

Jake *was* fast. Faster than he'd ever pulled an ace from his shirtsleeve. Faster than he'd ever drawn a gun under the table. Faster than a shot of rotgut whiskey. He handed the canteen to Billy. "Here, traitor, I hope it makes you puke."

"Long as I'm a *live* traitor." Billy took a long pull, then corked the canteen with his teeth, his gun never wavering from Jake's gut.

"Mind if I walk with you until I can't no more?"

"I don't trust you. Lay your guns on the ground."

"I guess I won't need 'em anymore." Jake drew his pistol, butt first, laid it at his feet, then looked expectantly at Billy.

Billy tapped his foot.

Jake smiled and removed a derringer from his boot.

The brothers stared at one another.

"And the one up your left sleeve that you don't think I know about."

"You were always sharper than I gave you credit for," Jake said.

"Go on," Billy said, "you lead off."

Jake started walking without a backward glance at his guns lying in the sand. He thought about asking Billy why he didn't keep them as a souvenir, but decided that *he* wouldn't want a keepsake from a moment like this. These were the moments in your life that you tried to forget. The moments where you weren't the man your Ma always thought you'd grow up to be. "How you gonna make a livin' now, Billy? I mean, you had the subtlest signs, and I played the cards. Easy money. We were the best team in the business. Why, you can spot a tick on a hound at fifty yards—no one ever suspected. Where else you gonna earn coin like that?"

"Anywhere they need a gun. And I'll tell ya, I ain't gonna be run outta town like this ever again."

"No. If'n you plan on makin' a livin' with them guns, you'll be stayin' in town, taking a dirt nap in the pine box hotel."

"Look at these guns."

Jake turned back to see Billy's twin Colts flash in the sun as he twirled them and holstered one, keeping the other on Jake.

"Guns like these, and they know I mean business."

"In all the towns we've ever visited, in all the conversations we've ever heard, when someone was lookin' to hire a gun, you ever hear them ask how shiny it was?" Jake grinned.

"Shut up, Jake."

Jake did, but kept smiling.

Billy took another long pull from the canteen.

"Better go easy," Jake said. "There was barely enough to get the two of us to the next town. You keep goin' like that, and you'll drop not long after me."

"Don't tell me how to drink my damn water." Billy waved the pistol for Jake to keep walking.

They walked in silence as they came out of the low desert into hills peppered with Joshua trees. Behind him, Jake heard the tread of Billy's boots on the dusty trail grow uneven.

"Maybe you should find a shady spot to make your peace with God," Billy said.

"Why do you say?"

"C-cause yer startin' to stumble and weave around."

Jake turned, not bothering to hide his smile. "One of us is, but it ain't me."

"What the...Jake, what'd you do?"

"Well, when you asked for the canteen, did you see the bush I was standin' next to?"

"What?"

"Jimson Weed, Billy, it was Jimson Weed. When I took a sip, I just slipped some right on into that canteen."

"You killed me!"

"No more than you killed me, Billy. That was the deal."

"I, I don't feel so good, and...and I'm seeing stuff."

"What stuff?"

"Ma? It... it's Ma. She's awful mad at me fer killin' you."

Jake did his best imitation of his mother's voice, "Well, Billy, you've been a very naughty boy."

"I'm sorry, Ma."

"Now Billy, you go right back and fetch Jake his guns this instant!"

"I…okay, Ma."

"Jake's grin broadened a notch. "And swear on my life, you'll never, ever, cross your only brother again!"

"I swear, Ma." He turned to Jake. His pupils were the size of silver dollars. "Let's go back and get your guns." He looked around. "Except I don't know where they are."

"That's all right, Billy. I remember. This way." He led Billy further down the trail, sometimes supporting him with a shoulder, other times just guiding him by the elbow. Sweat poured off of the hallucinating Billy.

"You look cold, Billy, take my coat, and… my hat's warmer than yours, better trade." Jake switched clothing as the unprotesting Billy flopped around, barely able to keep his feet.

Jake stood back and looked at his brother, then licked his palm and smoothed his brother's long hair down the back of his neck. In the right light, they could almost pass for twins. One last thing. "Those guns are weighing you down. Better let me hang on to them." Jake took the gun belt off of his delirious brother and buckled it onto himself.

When they came around a bend, Jake found the Sheriff blocking their way, sun at his back, hands on his guns.

"Sheriff," Jake nodded.

"You're late."

"We had a little hitch."

The Sheriff inclined his head toward Billy. "What's wrong with him?"

"That's the hitch. Had a little run-in with some Jimson Weed."

"The deal was, you brought him in alive."

"He is."

"Might not be for long. How much Jimson Weed?"

"Not much, just enough to get me out of a jam."

"All right, then. Go on, Billy. Get outta here."

"What about my horse and my money?"

"What about bringing me the infamous Jake Callaway alive? He's only worth half as much dead, so that comes out of your half. Let's see, One hundred dollars, minus half, plus a half for me... Say, Billy, I guess that leaves you with nothin'."

"What about the horse?" Jake nodded at the pair of animals grazing behind the Sheriff.

"I need that to get Jake back to town before he dies. I gotta get some water into him."

Jake went for Billy's guns, but fast as he was, the Sheriff was ready.

"Don't," the lawman said. "Lay them at your feet."

The bore of the Sheriff's pistol looked awful big from where Jake stood.

"Slow and careful-like. You wouldn't want me to mistake what you're doin'. That's a mistake that can't never be set right."

Jake laid Billy's pistols at his feet. "Can't you at least leave me a canteen of water?"

"Need it for your brother to dilute the poison? Now kick them pistols over here."

Jake did.

"Why don't you take his?" The Sheriff grabbed Billy, unslung the canteen from over Billy's shoulder, and threw it at Jake's feet. "Feels almost full. That ought to hold you." He picked up Billy's pistols and tucked them into his belt. Then picked Billy up by the waist and threw him over one of the horses. "Nice doing business with you."

Jake stared at the canteen lying in the dirt at his feet, then at the retreating figures of the Sheriff and his dying brother. He picked up the canteen, wondered how far a walk his guns were, and unscrewed the cap.

MOUNTAIN COFFEE

NEVADA, 1910

The kid shook with cold. Fear too, I reckoned. I made him about ten or a shade older. He stared at my ruined face, which, normally, I'd take offense to, but... well, the poor boy.

"You say you live over in Placerton?" I asked.

"Yes."

"And you got lost following your Pa home? Is that the way of it?"

The boy nodded.

"Sit by the fire. I'll fix you some coffee and tell you a story while we wait. The name's Joshua." I pinched my hat brim, pulling it down slightly.

He remained silent, not offering a name.

Best that way, I figured. "If'n your Pa ain't here by dawn, we'll leave a note, and I'll walk you around Dead Horse Ridge."

"My Pa can't read."

"Well, we'll leave an arrow then, so he knows which way we've gone."

The kid sat down, never taking his eyes from my face, but with manners enough not to ask about it.

"It's almost Christmas. Do you think your Pa will get you a present? Have you been a good boy?

"Yes," the kid looked down.

"You don't seem sure."

Without lifting his head, the kid raised his eyes. Definitely afraid. I s'pose if I'd seen me, a man with half a face, crouched by a spindly fire in the dead of night, I'd be afraid too. Then I remembered how it was. Just so. Best put the kid at ease.

"My Pa got me an orange once," I said, trying for a friendly smile with the working side of my mouth, "all the way from California. Juicy and delicious. But you are my present this year. You've brought me more joy than you can possibly imagine.

"Well," I poured water from my canteen into a pot. "I sure do get lonely out here. Nice to have someone to talk to, finally.

"Don't look so scared, kid. I've been in your situation once myself. See, me and Pa were out hunting mule deer." I set the pot on a glowing rock in the middle of my fire. "and for the second trip in a row, we were going home empty-handed. We stayed late, hoping for a last-minute kill as twilight turned to night. But darkness fell without so much as a rustle in the underbrush, and the mountain air turned cold.

"I began shaking uncontrollably in our blind. Pa sighed, rubbed my back and shoulders, and said. 'Your mother will have my head if you catch a chill. We'd best be heading downslope.'

"Pa made me eat the last of the jerked beef we'd brought, and we set out for home by lantern light. The way was long, and the trail dark. I tried to hide my fear, as Pa would always chide me at such times, 'there's nothin' on this mountain scarier than me, boy.'

"I had a hard time keeping up and cried out at the disappearing pool of yellow light, just a glowing dot. The silent forest came alive with noise, rustling in the trees, the crunch of dry pine needles. Shadows moved, dark on dark.

"Pa waited, and, when I stumbled back into the safety of the lamplight once more, he said, 'okay, boy. We'll take the Icy Creek shortcut. It'll get us down into the warmer air quicker.'"

The kid sat wide-eyed in the firelight. Frightened no doubt by my tale, but even more frightened to leave.

I must admit, I took some pleasure in affecting the boy this way, but I knew the coffee would warm and relax him. And I liked talking, telling my own tale of the mountain.

The kid didn't make a sound as I scooped the grounds into the already steaming water and continued.

"My Pa mistook my fear for cold. That was fine with me, as long as we got down out of the trees. Icy Creek burbled with menace like a witch's cauldron. The trail up there worked like a cattle shoot, fencing me in tangled barbs, gnarled trees, and darkness. Only one way to go. I had no trouble keeping up with Pa as we went down, my feet practically on his heels, as close to the lantern as I could get.

"Near the bottom of the mountain, a pinprick of orange light grew larger as we neared. Pa held a hand out, motioning me to wait alone. In the trees. In the dark. He went to see who's camp we'd be passing.

"I waited as long as I could, but the forest started rustlin' and scrapin' at me."

The kid shivered. Maybe he heard it out there, too.

"It was the scrapin' that got me. Sounded like a buck's horn on tree bark, 'cept this had rhythm, like a knife on a whetstone. Scrape. Scrape. Scrape." I ran my chipped nails along my pant leg three times.

The kid's eyes widened.

"I ran outta them trees like my ass was on fire and stood next to Pa. My elbow grazing his buckskin.

"The grizzled old man sat, warming his hands over a small fire of juniper and pinion twigs. When I burst out of the forest, he gave me a gap-toothed smile and his one good eye. See, his face was ruined, just like mine is now. Same three angry red lines runnin' temple to jaw crosswise. Only difference was, he wore an eyepatch hidin' *his* ruination. 'What's this? A child?' he asked.

"'My son,' Pa said. 'Joshua.'

"'He looks scared half to death,' the old man said. 'Come. Sit. Share my fire. You both look cold, too. I'll put some coffee on.' He turned to his pack, then stopped and looked me right in the eye. 'Did you hear something out there, boy? Did ya see shapes in the darkness?'

"I nodded and moved closer to Pa.

"'He's a sensitive boy,' Pa said and elbowed me away from his side.

"'I can see that he is,' the old man held my eye, 'don't worry, boy, I was a sensitive youngster once too, and look how I turned out.' He laughed and turned once again to his pack. 'I've got fine coffee in here somewhere, just the last little bit, but it always tastes better when there's someone to share it with.'

"'We've got to be gettin' on down the trail,' Pa said. 'Ma will be worried.'

"'Ye from over in Placerton?' the old man asked.

"'That's right,' Pa said.

"'Well, ye must've been in a bad way to take the Icy Creek Trail down. That's a long walk through the desert to get home, all the way 'round Dead Horse Ridge.'

"Pa looked down at me. 'Joshua was cold. I feared he'd get a chill, and his Ma would have my head.'

"The old man smiled. 'Well, better to warm up by the fire and get a little coffee in him and bring him home late than bring him home with a chill? Eh? Which do you think the missus would prefer?'

"Pa thought for a second, then nodded. 'Much obliged. Name's Lars Hansen.' Pa extended a hand.

"The old man came out of his pack with a small burlap sack, switched it to his off-hand, and shook with Pa. 'I'm Helmut Zeitgeist. Please, sit. The coffee won't take long. The coals are good and hot.'

"Pa and I sat cross-legged and watched as Helmut poured water into a pot and set it on a large rock that glowed red in the middle of the fire."

I stirred the coffee on my own fire and looked at the kid across from me.

He trembled, eyes wide.

"Do you want me to stop?" I grinned, straining the grounds through a brown cloth I kept for the purpose.

The kid shook his head and took the cup. He blew the steam off.

Drink the coffee, kid. Drink. I waited, and I made sure he took a good long gulp before I continued.

"We drank Helmut's coffee, but instead of perkin' us up, we felt...sleepy."

"'Have you ever heard of The Krampus, Joshua?' Helmut squinted at me with his one good eye.

"My tongue felt thick. I couldn't say nothin' back.

"'Well,' Helmut says, 'The Krampus is a demon, half-man, half-goat. He comes to take naughty children away into the woods to eat them, 'cept the ones he keeps to trap the others. I hope you've been good this year. You want to see Santa, don't you, Joshua? Not the Krampus.'

"My eyes felt heavy as two leaden sashes. Helmut kept talking. 'Did you know the first settlers named the Joshua trees after Joshua in the bible, raising his hands up to God?' Helmut lifted his eye patch like he could see out of the crinkled hole where his eye used to be. 'You ever raise your arms up to God like that? *Joshua*?'

"My lights went out.

"When I come to, straps bit into my arms. I couldn't move. Tree bark scraped into my back. I was lashed to a tree, see, arms raised up, just like Joshua from the bible. I started screaming, 'Pa, Pa help!' but he didn't answer.

"Helmut came close. He put his mouth to my ear. 'That's right, boy, scream, call it closer. End my bondage.' He sprinkled gold dust over my body and began shouting himself. "Come, Krampus. I have brought you a boy, covered in gold. My present to you. Now, release me!'

The kid across from me set his cup down. But his droopy eyes told me it was too late.

I kept on with my tale. "Sticks cracked loud in the dark forest. A terrible howling come out of the night. Sounded like a gut-shot mountain lion. Then I saw it, the Krampus, creepin' into the firelight. Its long spiral horns came to jagged, nasty ends.

Helmut backed away, sayin', 'Yes, yes, take the boy. He's juicy and delicious! Release me!'"

"The Krampus came close on back-jointed legs, like a horse. Its cloven hooves cracked sticks in half. Its forked tongue slithered out and licked tar-black lips. Its breath stank of old death. Its sticky saliva burned like acid as it licked the gold from my face.

"'You are released, Helmut,' it growled. 'I take the boy in your place.' The Krampus raised a three-fingered claw, then brought it down, ripping me open…." I was so wrapped up tellin' my tale I didn't notice the kid.

He swayed drunkenly, too close to the fire.

I dashed over, afraid he'd fall in. Afraid he'd ruin my present.

"How was the coffee, kid?"

OTHER TITLES BY LEN M. RUTH

The Pull

The Demons Within Book 1

The Unrecoverd

Smiling Flu book 1

Rachael's Apocalypse Diary

a Smiling Flu companion story

Turn the page for a sneak peek at

Len M. Ruth's

Genre busting new novel

To keep up with the latest releases from Len M. Ruth check out his website at https://lenmruth.com.

THE UNRECOVERED

CHAPTER 1, DESTINATION IDAHO

Jamie strained for a glimpse of the approaching fires in the dusty orange sky to the west. The forest on the other side of the cornfields wasn't visible through the kitchen window, but she could smell fire on the breeze that rustled the curtains.

Ed's footsteps creaked down the stairs.

She swept aside a few of the coupons littering the kitchen table, set her coffee down, and sat gazing at them with a mix of disdain and resignation.

"Sky's a funny color," she said as Ed shuffled past her.

"Smoke from the fires," he mumbled.

She watched him take the Laetanol bottle down from atop the fridge and tap one into his calloused hand. He filled a red jelly glass from the tap, swallowed the pill, then stared out the window just as Jamie had moments before.

"Do you think those are working?" She clipped a coupon for cornflakes from the circular and laid it on the growing pile.

"Do you?"

"I suppose," she paused, looking at his muscular arms and back silhouetted against the orange sky. "You don't seem as sad."

"Yeah," he said, "I don't feel as sad."

"So that's it. You gonna do it?" she asked, changing the

subject. His depression was a rabbit hole she'd rather not go down this morning.

"Yeah." Ed turned from the window and rested the small of his back on the counter. "The harvester's all fueled up."

"It's a lot of money to lose," she said, returning her attention to her coupons.

"We talked about this." Ed sighed. "I can still sell the early corn. We'll lose about ten percent on that acreage. Better that than lose it all to the fire. Forest Service says it should create a good fire break. After I harvest, they'll come in and burn the stalks. Ted is doing the same to his fields right now."

"How long will you be?"

"Midnight, I figure." He picked up the thermos and lunch bag she'd prepared for him.

Jamie got up and stopped him at the door. "I love you." She put her arms around his sunburned neck and felt the hard muscle of his shoulders under her slender fingers. She did love him. Didn't she? Or was it the idea of him? The ghost of Ed, the one she'd married, was bright and full of promise. A young college student on the rise like herself. And she'd been swept away by their love like solar wind. Swept years later to his parent's farm in Destination, Idaho, clipping coupons and putting up with his drinking.

"I love you too." He put his arms around her.

The lunch bag and thermos pressed against her back.

"It's going to be alright, Jamie." He kissed her.

Jamie accepted the kiss, tasting the familiar tang of vodka. She wondered as she kissed him back if he meant the crops, the farm, the fire, their marriage? There were so many things that were not all right.

"Ew," came a small playful voice, "can I go outside?"

Jamie turned to see Aella standing in the doorway to the dining room.

As Aella ran the back of her hand across her nose, her fingers brushed the tips of long brown ringlets that framed her face and set them jiggling.

"Go blow your nose. You're twelve years old. You shouldn't have to be told," Jamie said. "you're not getting sick, are you?"

"No," Aella said over her shoulder as she went off in search of a tissue.

"Probably just all the smoke in the air," Ed said.

"I hope that's all. I don't want her sick for the big trip tomorrow." Jamie rested her head on Ed's chest and slipped her hands into the back pockets of his jeans. "I wish I could go with her."

"She'll be in good hands," Ed said, "She's got who? Cheryl Thompson, plus three other chaperones from her troop. She sold a lot of cookies to get there. Can't keep her home now."

"I know. I just wish I could share the wonder with her. I always wanted to see the Smithsonian and the Lincoln Memorial."

"I wish I could earn enough money so you didn't have to wait tables. Take us on a real vacation. Speaking of money, I've got to get that harvester rolling before we lose everything."

"OK," Jamie said. She kissed his cheek and watched him go down the steps and around the side of the house.

"Can I go out now?" Aella asked, tossing a tissue into the trash.

"You sure you feel OK?" Jamie asked, looking her over.

"I'm sure." Aella gave her mother a sweet smile.

Jamie let out a breath. "OK, as long as you are all packed."

"Yup, all packed."

"Stay around the yard. I don't want you wandering off into the fields with that fire so close."

"It won't come here. Dad said. Isn't that where he went? To harvest the fields on the edge of the woods?"

"Yes, yes. OK, go on, and don't get your new sneakers muddy before the trip."

"OK." Aella crossed the kitchen. The screen door made a "graaanngg" sound as she opened it.

"And don't let the—" CLACK "—screen door slam." Jamie shook her head and went back to her coupons.

"Mom, the eclipse is happening!" Aella's voice floated in through the screen door a few minutes later.

Jamie went to the window. "I totally forgot about it. Don't stare at it."

"I *know*."

"I'll bring out those special glasses."

Jamie fetched the cardboard-framed plastic lenses and joined Aella in the yard. After making sure Aella put them on, Jamie put on her own and stared up at the cosmic spectacle.

Smoke wafted low out of the cornfields and swirled around them. It barely registered through their dark glasses, just a faint gray shadow, but from the corner of her eye, Jamie could see its faint pink color. The swirling vapor vanished as quickly as it came, leaving a chemical taste on her tongue. Strange smoke. What the hell burned to make that shit? She shrugged it off and turned her attention back to the eclipse. The moon slid perfectly across the sun, creating the fiery halo of totality.